MURDER BY THE GLASS
Cocktail Mysteries

Edited by Teresa Inge and Yvonne Saxon

Untreed
Reads

Murder by the Glass—Cocktail Mysteries
Edited by Teresa Inge and Yvonne Saxon

Cover Copyright 2021 by Untreed Reads Publishing
Cover Design by Ginny Glass

"A Taste of Murder" by Alan Orloff
"Murder on Tap" by Teresa Inge
"Grape Minds Drink Alike" by Allie Marie
"Revenge on the Rocks" by Betsy Ashton
"Swiping Right" by Kristin Kisska
"Malbec Gold" by Frances Aylor
"EverUs" by K.L. Murphy
"The Nightcap" by Diane Fanning
"Bucket List Dreams" by Debra H. Goldstein
"Zero Hour" by Josh Pachter
"Chimera" by Libby Hall
"Out of Commission" by Heather Weidner
"Brayking Glass" by Eleanor Cawood Jones
"How Do You Mend a Broken Heart?" by Maggie King
"Here's to You, Mrs. Robinson" by Teresa Inge
"From Whiskey to Wine" by Shawn Reilly Simmons
"The Good Citizen" by Mary Dutta
"Fly Away Gourmet" by Maria Hudgins

ISBN-13: 978-1-94913-549-7

Also available in ebook format.

Published by Untreed Reads, LLC
506 Kansas Street, San Francisco, CA 94107
www.untreedreads.com

Printed in the United States of America.

Publisher's Note
This is a work of fiction. Names, characters, places, and incidents either are the product of the author's imagination or are used fictitiously, and any resemblance to actual persons, living or dead, business establishments, events, or locales is entirely coincidental.

The publisher does not have any control over and does not assume any responsibility for author or third-party websites or their content.

Contents

INTRODUCTION

The idea for *Murder by the Glass* came about when anthology coordinators, Teresa Inge and Heather Weidner met for dinner and drinks to brainstorm a mysterious beverage anthology, featuring cocktails, murder, and a glass.

After a few glasses of wine, the authors created *Murder by the Glass: Cocktail Mysteries* by seventeen established authors, each blending a baffling mystery, a glass, and a murder.

A TASTE OF MURDER
by Alan Orloff

Detective Stephen Baker knelt next to the body, observing without touching. No obvious signs of external violence. No bloody knife sticking out of the victim's barrel chest. No gunshot wound. No bashed-in skull.

He'd leave it to the Medical Examiner to determine the cause of death, but Baker figured the victim had been poisoned. Call it an experienced detective's hunch. Of course, the telltale smell of bitter almonds associated with cyanide helped support his theory.

"Hey, Baker." Vin Cooper, filling in for Baker's regular partner, had materialized at his side.

Baker rose, knees cracking. He was of a certain vintage and on days like today, he was aging rapidly. "Yeah?"

Cooper held up an evidence bag containing a small empty vial. "Think we got the cause of death. I gave it a sniff before I bagged it. Cyanide."

Baker silently congratulated himself. "Where did you find it?"

"On the floor. Inside the tasting room. Someone must have dumped it into the victim's glass and tossed it on the floor."

"Vic's name is Woody Tannenbaum. Not a pleasant way to go."

"There are worse ways," Cooper said with an acidic tone. "A wine tasting as part of the pre-wedding festivities? Kinda fruity, huh? Whatever happened to bachelor parties? Instead of strippers, we got sippers!"

Cretin. Baker hated it when his regular partner took a vacation. "Did you separate the witnesses?"

"I did, but don't you mean *suspects*?" Cooper arched an eyebrow.

Sometimes a fine line. "Perhaps you're right. But let's not jump to any conclusions. We're going to do it all by the book, Vin. I'll question the witnesses, starting with the groom. You keep looking for physical evidence, okay?"

1

Cooper narrowed his eyes, and Baker knew he didn't like getting relegated to the background. But Baker was the senior detective, so he called the shots.

*

Baker set up shop in a dingy back room of Happy Days Vineyards, boxes of wine stacked against one wall. A single overhead bare bulb struggled to illuminate the small space. To him, the oak-paneled room resembled an interrogation room from some old black-and-white detective movie.

Sitting across a cluttered table, the groom, Evan Hunter, wore a silky burgundy shirt which made his hollow expression even starker in the dim light. "Who would want to kill Woody?"

"Who said anybody killed him?" Baker asked.

"You're homicide detectives, so I assumed. And he was in perfect health, until..."

"Until he died?" Baker tried to keep his sarcasm in reserve. "Just tell me what happened, and please don't filter it." Baker clicked his ballpoint pen open, ready to take notes, even though he had his phone recording the entire interview.

"We were tasting wines, having fun, nothing unusual at all. Woody said he wasn't feeling well and got up to use the restroom. When he didn't come back after about fifteen minutes, I went to see what was going on and found him on the floor. That's all."

"And he was dead?"

Hunter gulped. "Yes."

"Did you get along with Tannenbaum?"

"Woody was my best friend. My *Best Man*. Yes, I got along with him. And if you're implying I had something to do with this, you're way off base. We've known each other since seventh grade."

"Okay, if you didn't kill him, who did?"

Hunter shook his head slowly. "How would I know?"

"It seems that someone in your little wedding party killed him. Care to offer an opinion?"

"No. No. None of us would have killed him." Something flashed behind Hunter's mask of grief.

"So, no theories?"

Baker waited for an answer, but Hunter stared at him blankly. Baker could practically see the gears working behind his angular pretty-boy face. He offered a weak smile and kept his mouth shut. More often than not a witness filled the silence.

It didn't take long before Hunter caved. "Well..." He glanced around then leaned in close, as if someone would overhear them. "I heard Woody and Karl arguing, right after we arrived."

"Karl Trent? The manager here?"

"Yes. He and Woody were college roommates. Woody reached out to Karl to set this whole thing up. In fact, Karl offered to throw a big shindig here, but we decided to make it more intimate. Thought we'd have a nicer time, just the four of us getting the VIP treatment. Some nice time." Hunter's eyes got misty, then he turned and stared at the wall.

"What were they arguing about?"

After a moment, Hunter swiveled around, wiped his eyes dry. "Something about money. About this winery. Karl is a part owner, and a couple years ago, he invited Woody to invest in it too."

"Walk me through what you saw, what you heard."

"I was in the breezeway heading toward the restroom when I caught sight of them on the back patio, near one of those large rustic vats. It looked like Woody was about to attack Karl, who seemed quite defensive. Karl started moving backward, but Woody grabbed his arm and wouldn't let go. Evidently, they heard someone coming from the other corner of the patio, because Woody released Karl before they could finish. Karl said something—tasteless, judging by Woody's expression—and then stormed off. When Karl started pouring our wines later, everything seemed normal, so maybe they'd resolved their issue."

Or maybe not.

*

A big man, more beefy than brawny, Karl Trent overflowed the standard-sized chair across the table from Baker. He wore a forest-green flat cap, with the initials of the winery, HDV, subtly embroidered on one side of the brim.

Baker jumped right in. "So you went to school with the victim?"

"That's right." Trent's gaze flitted around the small space, as if he'd never seen his own back supply room before.

"Get along?"

"With Woody? Sure. Back then, and now, too. I arranged this Champagne and Caviar brunch for him. Woody wanted everything to go smoothly for his buddy." His face sagged.

"Can you tell me about the tasting? How did things unfold?"

"Once everyone arrived, we got them set up in the VIP room. I started by explaining how the tasting would go, just like I always do. We started with some appetizers and caviar, along with the first selections of wine. Usually a staffer handles all the serving and pouring, but since I knew Woody, I took care of it all. No way did I want it to tank."

"Okay. Anything seem out of the ordinary?"

Trent shook his head. "Nope. They enjoyed the food, enjoyed the wine. I got the feeling they didn't care so much about all the details of the wine, so I didn't go into any dense explanations. Kept it light. Everyone seemed to be having a fine time, until... Well, you know."

Baker nodded solemnly. "Do you know anyone who was having issues with Woody? Anyone who might want to harm him?"

Trent pursed his fleshy lips. "Nope. People liked him. Seemed to gravitate toward him. He could be very charming. Ask the ladies."

"You ever have an issue with him?"

"Ever? Sure. Nothing major though. Just your typical disagreements. Now and then."

"Have a *disagreement* with him today?"

Trent smiled, mouth only, no eyes. "Okay, I get it. I argued with Woody so I must have killed him." He held out his hands, wrists together. "Slap the cuffs on me, Holmes, you've solved the case."

"Is that a confession?"

Trent jerked his hands back quickly causing his flabby forearms to jiggle. "No way. I didn't kill Woody. He was my bro. I wouldn't hurt him."

"What were you arguing about?"

Trent kept his lips pressed together.

"If you don't tell me, you know I'm going to think it was something serious. Something worth killing for."

He exhaled. "Business, all business. Woody bought into this place a couple of years ago, when we needed a cash infusion. He thought he had a nose for this business. At the time, he agreed to be a silent partner, but lately, he's been a lot less quiet about things. We had a small difference about an ownership issue."

"My witness described it as more than a *small* difference."

"Woody could be dramatic." Trent shrugged. "Besides, we had disagreements like that frequently." As soon as he said it, Trent blanched, realizing he wasn't helping his case. "You know what I mean. Trust me, there's nothing to it. And more importantly, I didn't kill Woody."

"Okay, then. Who did?"

"I've been racking my brain, trying to come up with a plausible suspect, but I got nothing." One of Trent's eyebrows wiggled. "Although I do know someone who owes him some money."

"Oh?"

"Yeah. Woody wanted to buy more of the business—that's what we were arguing about. I was hesitant, but he insisted. He said something like, quote, 'As soon as I get repaid, I'll be in a position to buy a bigger stake in this business.'"

"Did he say who owed him? Did he say how much?"

Trent's fidgeting increased. His gaze landed everywhere, except on Baker. Finally, he exhaled. "I hate to incriminate anyone, but I guess you'll find out eventually. It was Rose. She owed him money. She owed him thirty large."

*

Rose Harrison's delicate floral perfume wafted across the small interview room. Lush hair cascaded over her shoulders. She wore a berry-colored sheath dress that accentuated her full-bodied figure, and sat with her hands folded in her lap, staring at Baker with steely eyes. "For the record, I did not kill Woody."

"I never said you did." Baker tapped his notebook with his pen. "Although I understand that you owed him a rather large sum of money."

A blush spread across her face. "That's right. Thirty thousand dollars. I was about to pay him back, however. Wipe the slate clean."

"Why did you borrow the money?"

"I lost my job, and I needed some cash to get me through. Woody was kind enough to help me out."

"From the goodness of his heart?"

With two fingers she swirled her hair. "Woody could be very cooperative. A nice guy."

"I'm a nice guy, too. Doesn't mean I'd pony up thirty thousand dollars." Baker had a feeling there was more to the story. Of course, there usually was. And usually it had a personal angle. "Were you involved with him?"

"Involved?" Rose uncrossed and recrossed her legs in the other direction.

"Romantically involved. Were you dating him, Ms. Harrison?"

She swallowed. Opened her mouth, snapped it shut. Then her features seemed to melt, and she gave Baker a curt nod. "For about nine months. Ended about a year ago."

"And who ended it?"

A pause. "It was mutual."

Baker figured that anytime someone said a break-up was mutual, they were the one who got dumped. "Did you harbor any ill will toward him?"

"No. Like I said, the breakup was mutual. And he'd loaned me money, so really, I was grateful to him."

"Okay, then. You have any thoughts about who might want to see Woody dead?"

Rose blushed again, then a few tears formed in the corner of her eyes. "She would not have killed him. No way."

"Who are you talking about?"

"There is no way in the world Sherry would have killed Woody. She's not vindictive like that."

"What motive would Sherry have to kill Woody?"

"Because he hopped from my bed into hers."

"Are you telling me that Woody and the bride had a fling?"

"A fling sounds like a one-night stand. No, this wasn't 'any storm in a port.' Woody and Sherry had an organic thing. Went on for six months or so. Maybe longer."

"Went on. How long has it been over?"

Rose grimaced. "About two weeks."

"Don't tell me, the break-up was mutual."

"Oh no, not at all. She dumped him, and boy, was he pissed!" she said, with a blend of horror and glee in her voice.

*

The bride-to-be, Sherry Green, looked anything but radiant. She slumped in her chair and dabbed her red eyes with a scrunched-up tissue. As she did, she started to sob uncontrollably.

"Just breathe." Baker waited for Sherry to regain control, and when she did, he slipped into his softest voice. "Terrible thing to happen on your wedding weekend. So sorry about that."

Sherry gave a final snuffle and moved her tissue from eyes to nose. "Yes. Thank you. Do you know what happened? I mean, why would anyone want to kill Woody? He was such a sweet person. Never bitter at all."

"Why do you think?"

"I honestly have no idea."

"Well, we've talked to everyone involved, and a few possible theories have come up."

"Really?" She sounded surprised, but her eyes told a different story.

"Yes. Seems Woody was quite a..." He let his sentence ferment in the air, like the aroma of spilled wine.

"What? Quite a what?"

Player? Baker cleared his throat. "Well, why don't you describe him for me?"

A pause. A nod. "Well, sure. Woody was a complex, brilliant man, but he has his faults. *Had* his faults." Another sniffle. "Don't we all? But—"

Baker interrupted. "Maybe you could describe them. His faults, I mean."

"Okay, I guess. He was a bit...egocentric, maybe. Liked things his own way. Didn't always obey the rules. But deep down, he was a gentle, caring guy."

"Sounds like you knew him pretty well."

"Well, uh, sure. He is—was—Evan's best friend." Something caught in her voice.

"Uh huh. I got the idea that you knew him a little better than that."

Sherry stared at him, wringing her hands. "I'm not sure what you heard exactly, but you can't believe everything you hear."

"What do you imagine I heard?"

Her tone hardened. "I see what you're doing here."

"Just trying to get to the truth."

She stared into her lap, then raised her head and met Baker's eyes. "Okay, I'll spill. Full disclosure. But I ask one favor. Can you please keep this just between us?"

"This is an official police investigation, Ms. Green." Baker leaned in, modulated his voice again. Honey, not vinegar. "But I promise to do the best I can. I get no joy wrecking people's lives."

"Very well. I...I was seeing Woody."

"Romantically?"

"Yes. I'm not proud of myself, Detective, but like I said, Woody had that *je ne sais quoi*. He was kind of a hybrid—he could be bold, aggressive. And decadent. But he also had depth and would occasionally act mature beyond his years."

"How long had this been going on?"

"Eight months. Up until a couple of weeks ago. I finally realized that I was going to screw up my entire life if I didn't end it. You see, I love Evan very much, and Woody...well, every woman had a crush on him, but he wasn't the kind of guy you marry. Too unreliable. I had the feeling that at any moment, he could take flight."

"What was his reaction when you broke it off?"

"Woody was gentle—most of the time. But he had a hot temper, although he kept it bottled up most of the time. To say he wasn't happy would be an understatement."

"Did he threaten you?"

"How do you mean?"

"Did he threaten to tell your fiancé, for instance?"

Sherry tilted her head. "Rose told you that, didn't she?"

"I don't divulge my sources."

"She blabbed. That bitch. After all the secrets I've kept for that tart?"

"Did he? Threaten to expose the affair?"

"Yes."

"And what was your response?"

"Honestly? I told him that if he ruined my life by telling Evan, I'd kill him."

"Is that a confession?" Baker rarely asked that question, and now, twice in one afternoon.

"Oh, please, I didn't kill Woody. I loved him. And I don't know who would."

"Are you aware that your maid of honor also had a relationship with the deceased?"

Sherry waved her hand in the air dismissively. "That was old news. They'd both moved on. Rose didn't mind at all. She certainly had no reason to want Woody dead, trust me."

"What about your fiancé? Did he know about your affair?"

Another wave of the hand, but not as forcefully. "He would never kill Woody. Evan's not the jealous type."

"You didn't exactly answer my question."

She paused, for what seemed like a full sixty seconds. "I don't know. I never told him, and he never asked me." Another long pause. "But he may have suspected."

*

Baker and Cooper conferred in the impromptu interrogation room.

"Here's a quick recap. We got four witnesses who are also suspects, and, on balance, they all seem to have motives. What a fiasco!" Baker ran a hand through his hair. Why couldn't he have gotten a real confession? It would have made things *so* much simpler. "The bride was having an affair with the victim, so the groom would have a pretty darn good reason to kill him. And the victim had threatened to expose the affair to the groom unless the bride kept it going, so she also had a good reason to want him silenced."

"Oh boy," Cooper said. "Our victim was plonking the bride? Kinda makes you wonder why people want to be monogamous."

"It gets better. The maid-of-honor also had a romantic

relationship with the deceased until he split. I got the feeling she wasn't very happy about that break-up. Plus she owed him money—to the tune of thirty thousand dollars. Get rid of him, get rid of her debt."

"Rose? The racy one with supple skin who dresses foxy? Spicy dress, spiky heels?"

"Must you be so...earthy?"

"Just calling it like I see it," Cooper said.

"And there's more than just the love triangle. Hunter saw the manager, Trent, arguing with the victim before the tasting began. Seems they were in business together and disagreed on some things. From what Hunter described, they almost came to blows. Trent had the means—he could easily have spiked Woody's wine."

A thought bubbled up from the depths of Baker's mind. "You still got the vial?"

"I gave it to the tech. But I took a picture first. That do?"

"Lemme see it."

Cooper called it up on his phone, showed it to Baker.

He examined the photo for a moment. "Forward the photo to me, will you? I've got an idea. You and I will tell each of the suspects one piece of information. You note their response, and I'll note their reaction."

Baker explained his plan which drew another smirk from Cooper.

"Sounds devious. My kind of questioning. I knew you'd come around eventually," Cooper said.

Baker allowed himself a small smile. "Hopefully, someone will pour their heart out and it will yield results."

*

After they'd spoken with each suspect, Baker gathered everyone together in the tasting room, in *reveal-the-killer-in-the-parlor style* straight out of an Agatha Christie novel.

Off to one side, Sherry and Hunter bickered. Somehow news of the bride's infidelities must have made its way to the groom. Baker cleared his throat, but they kept on arguing. He raised his voice. "May I have everyone's attention?"

Hunter swung around to face Baker, agitation evident. "What's going on? Do you think this is some kind of sick game?"

"On the contrary," Baker said. "I've got a pretty good idea who committed the crime. Before I begin, though, would anyone like to confess? It might make things go a little easier on you." He made eye contact with each suspect.

The suspects exchanged glances, but no one spilled their guts.

"Okay, then. Let's proceed." Baker consulted an index card he'd pulled from his pocket. "Detective Cooper and I told you all the same piece of information, namely that we were able to lift a fingerprint from the vial of poison, and that we would know definitively who the killer was very shortly."

He paused and looked up. Everyone was staring at him intently, waiting for the big reveal. "Here are the responses we got. Three of you said something to the effect of 'it's not mine' or 'thank goodness.' Each response was accompanied by a look of anger. Anger that someone had murdered their friend. However, one person responded by saying, quote, 'Really? From that tiny vial?' And that person had a look on their face that could only be described as *petrified*."

Now, the suspects examined each other with suspicion, trying to discern the outlier.

Baker held up his phone displaying the picture of the vial. "You might not be able to see the vial in this photo, but it's quite small. Highly improbable that we could lift a usable print from it. But we hadn't shown the vial to anyone, so the only person who knew how tiny it was, and how extremely difficult it would be to get a print from, would have to be the killer."

Now Baker paused, giving the moment the weight it deserved. "Isn't that right, Rose?"

All attention shifted to Rose. She tried to maintain a poker face, but it soured quickly. "It was practically self-defense. Woody threatened to destroy me, and I knew him well enough to know that he would. I tried talking to him, pleading with him, but he demanded that I pay him back the money I owed him threefold, even though that wasn't part of the deal. Pure blackmail. I had no choice, it was either him or me." She put her head in her hands and started sobbing.

Everyone else sat there, shocked.

But only for a moment. Then the bride and groom launched back into their heated argument. Baker figured there wasn't going to be any wedding, that weekend, or any weekend, not after what had transpired. There'd be no walk down the aisle, no bouquet to catch.

No bottle of champagne to toast their happy union.

He glanced at the couple again. Hunter's face was so red and his tone so angry that Baker figured it was just a matter of moments until the day had its fitting end.

The groom was about to pop his cork.

MURDER ON TAP
by Teresa Inge

Cassidy "Cass" Kennedy entered the crowded Belmar bar. Her lanyard swayed back and forth, while her conference bag slid down her shoulder. She approached her friends. "How were your panels?"

"We had hoggers." Kym Mansfield put her fingers in quotes.

Valinda Murray nodded.

Cass adjusted her bag and pushed her glasses into her long blond curls. "They are the worst." She referred to authors who hog panels. The three authors were veterans at the annual mystery writers conference "Murder at the Banks" in the OBX, the Outer Banks of North Carolina, a spit of land between the Atlantic Ocean and the Pamlico Sound, and a mecca for beach vacationers.

Cass glanced at Valinda's glass of Rosé wine. "That looks good."

She headed to the bar with Kym and Valinda behind her.

"Rosé?" asked the handsome bartender.

"You remembered?" Cass was flattered.

"Goes with the job. Rosé for you as well?" He nodded toward Kym.

"Yes."

As Matt grabbed two glasses, Cass faced Kym and Valinda. "Not sure if I'm impressed that he remembers what we drink, or if it means we're drunks."

Matt handed the women their wine. "I'll add it to your room tab."

"He provides good service." Cass sipped the refreshing wine.

"That's not all he provides," Kym suggested.

"What do you mean?" Cass said.

Kym wiggled her finger to move closer. "I can't say this too loud, but after I had wine at the bar last night, Matt here offered to bring a bottle to my room."

Cass and Valinda's mouths flew open.

"Personal room service?" Cass asked.

"With a smile!"

"Did you take him up on the offer?" Valinda asked.

"Hell no."

"Don't all look at once, but Matt knows the beverage choice for women of a certain age," Cass pointed out.

The women turned their heads toward Matt.

"I said don't all look at once."

"You think he's running a racket?" Valinda asked.

The three women drank their wine while observing Matt's flirtatious interactions with only pretty, female authors. After a full day of panels and book signings, the bar served as a gathering spot for authors.

"He'll eventually get caught," Cass offered.

"Not to change the subject, but where are we going for dinner?" Kym asked.

Before the women could respond, Oakley Ray, writer of historical short stories and conference coordinator, approached the group. Madeline Larue and Ava Ellery, both mystery writers and conference helpers, dogged her heels.

"Hello, ladies. I caught your panels today," Oakley said. "Great discussion on historical women, Cass. I suggest you show two items from your grandmother's collection instead of six. And Valinda, better to give the audience visuals of the sand between your toes for your beach series." Oakley adjusted her lanyard.

Cass and Valinda glared at Oakley.

"Kym. You need to speak up on the panel."

After an awkward silence, Cass asked. "Is there something you need, Oakley?"

"A group of us are going to Banks Seafood for dinner if you want to join."

Madeline faced Cass. "Other nominees are attending." Madeline referred to authors nominated for awards at the banquet tomorrow night. Cass had been nominated for the Best Historical Novel.

Matt approached Oakley. "Here's your L'Amour Chardonnay."

Oakley grabbed the glass.

"I'll add it to your tab." He walked back to the bar. "Matt is amazing. He knows I only drink L'Amour."

"He sure is," Kym agreed.

"We're meeting in the lobby at six-thirty," Oakley said. "We'll walk to the restaurant together. I hope you can make it." Oakley and the two women disappeared into a sea of mystery authors.

"Are we going?" Kym asked.

"Oakley is a snob. Why did she invite us anyway?" Cass asked.

"You don't know?"

Cass shrugged.

"Word on the mystery street is that your book *Murder at the Cavalier* may win tomorrow night."

"There's no way of knowing who will win until it's announced."

"True. But you have as good a chance as the rest of the nominees," Kym said. "I say we go to dinner with them to get out of the hotel."

"I'm in. But don't seat me next to Oakley."

Back in her room, Cass finished edits to her next book. She contacted her daughter back home in Chesapeake, Virginia. Her daughter was her biggest supporter of her writing career.

After retiring from a financial firm, Cass began writing historical mysteries full time. As a child, her grandmother shared stories of her travels, jewelry, and clothing which impressed Cass.

Recently, her grandmother gave her items to share during Cass's author talks.

After dressing in white shorts and a black top with a sexy vibe, Cass headed to the lobby. She took in the Belmar's coastal décor.

Ocean hues, blue and white casual furniture, and beachy art canvasses made a relaxed atmosphere. Cass loved the hotel. She glanced around for Valinda and Kym but did not see them. Since she was early, she walked to the bar and sat down. Matt was working.

"Rosé?" His handsome looks could make any woman give in to his charm.

She nodded. "You work a lot."

He poured the wine into a glass. "Uh...yeah. We're short bartenders for the conference so I'm on double shifts."

"We pretty much take over the hotel."

"Anything else I can get you?"

"Not right now."

Cass sipped her wine. Two women sat beside her.

Matt approached them. "Chardonnay?"

"You got it."

"He's handsome," one of the women said.

"He's young enough to be your son," the other woman responded.

Matt brought their wine. "Cheers, ladies!"

A few minutes later, an attractive blond in her fifties sat at the end of the bar. Cass recognized her as Kathryn Grayson, a historical fiction writer on her panel tomorrow. Matt brought a bottle of Blushing Blush wine and poured her a glass. While placing a bowl of trail mix on the counter, Matt spoke in a low voice. Kathryn slipped something into his hand. Cass was curious since she could not see what it was nor hear their conversation.

"Cass. You coming?" Valinda asked. "Cass. You coming to dinner?"

Cass turned to see Valinda and Kym behind her.

She was so engrossed in the hand exchange she forgot about dinner. She sipped her wine and waved good-bye to Matt.

"What was that about?" Kym asked.

"I had a few minutes to spare so I came to the bar."

"Uh-huh." Valinda remarked.

They met the group in the lobby and walked to the restaurant. Oakley led the way along Virginia Dare Trail at Milepost 8.5. Mileposts helped tourists find restaurants, shopping, and businesses. Once inside, Cass breathed in the seafood aroma. Attending the conference had its advantages, and Banks Seafood was one of them.

"This way ladies, and Richard!" Oakley waved her hand toward a back table. Richard Morris, the only male in the group, was best friends with Oakley. They had produced award-winning mystery anthologies together.

"Sit where you want!" Oakley shouted over the noise.

Since Valinda and Kym were ahead of her, Cass placed her hand on the chair next to Richard. "May I?"

"Of course."

She squeezed into the narrow space.

"Congrats on your nomination. Feels good, huh?"

Cass wasn't sure if he meant his knee crammed against her leg or her nomination. She assumed the latter. "Uh...yeah. It does."

Two red-headed women approached the table to take drink and dinner orders.

After receiving the beverages, Oakley approached Cass and Richard with a glass of wine.

"L'Amour wine?" Richard asked.

She nodded. "I see you two are cozy."

"Always a kind word."

"Now, is that nice to say to your best friend?" Oakley smirked.

Richard raised his glass of blush wine.

Cass assumed they had a love-hate relationship.

"By the way, did you catch Richard's and my anthologies panel?" Oakley asked Cass.

"Uh...no."

"Pity. You could have learned how to present items properly."

Cass sipped her wine. "Actually, I heard the items were not authentic."

Richard raised his blond eyebrows.

Oakley extended her glass toward Cass. "Who said that?"

"Two women in the vendor's room."

"Who were they?" Oakley's eyes crossed.

"I have no clue."

"As much as I do for the authors by placing them on panels." Oakley raised her voice. "Most of them don't even deserve a panel."

The attendees at the table became quiet.

Richard whispered to Oakley.

"Well...everyone has their opinion." She returned to her seat.

After dinner, Cass teamed up with Valinda and Kym on the walk back to the hotel.

"Oakley was furious," Kym said as they hung back from the group.

"I'd had enough of her comments about my grandmother's items."

The women crossed the street toward the Belmar and entered the bar.

"Matt is still working," Kym pointed out.

"He's doing double shifts since they are short on bartenders," Cass said.

"And how do you know that?" Valinda grabbed lipstick from her clutch and applied it.

"He told me earlier."

In record time, Matt appeared with a tray of wine. "I'll add it to your tab." They thanked him and sipped their beverages.

Within thirty minutes, the bar was filled with authors returning from dinner. Oakley approached the women.

"Where are your minions?" Kym asked.

"Very funny." Oakley faced Cass. "I want to know who said that about my panel."

Cass tightened the grip on her glass. "I told you I don't know."

"If you find out, report it to me immediately." Oakley stormed off.

"She's full of herself," Valinda said.

Richard approached. "May I introduce Kathryn Grayson. She is a nominee in the same category as Cass." Richard held a glass of Scotch.

The women congratulated Kathryn.

"You weren't at dinner this evening with the other nominees," Cass said.

"I had an appointment. Richard filled me in."

"Ready for our panel tomorrow?" Cass asked.

"I'm looking forward to it."

After a few minutes, Richard pulled Cass to the side. "Oakley is upset about your remark at dinner. It would be best to apologize."

"For what?"

"As her best friend, I recommend telling her you're sorry for what the women said. It would make all of our lives better for the rest of the conference."

"Appease her?"

"Yes."

"She can dish it out but can't take it."

Richard grabbed Kathryn's arm and off they went to suck up to other authors.

Valinda and Kym moved toward Cass. "You okay?" they said.

"Yeah. I'm ready for bed. Big day tomorrow. The author's breakfast and photo shoot start at seven, then panels, signings, and the banquet."

The women said goodnight and headed to their rooms.

Cass stepped onto her balcony, enjoying the ocean breeze. She checked social media. The authors who attended the event each year in May flooded social media with photos. She put on yoga pants, a t-shirt, and headed to bed.

The next morning, Cass dressed in white, slim fit capris and a blush, silk blouse. She placed her grandmother's items in her bag, slipped on her lanyard, and walked to the lobby.

"Morning!" Richard was cheery.

Cass looked up from her phone. "Morning."

"Did you talk to Oakley?"

"No."

"Here's your chance. She's walking toward us."

"Morning, Oak. Aren't you speaking at the author's breakfast shortly?" Richard asked.

"On my way there now. Just wanted a quick word with Cass."

Cass frowned.

"I need coffee. Good luck," he whispered to Cass and walked away.

"I overreacted last night. As mentioned before, I do a lot for the attendees and get little in return." Oakley lowered her lip.

Cass was surprised Oakley was vulnerable.

"I'm sorry that happened."

"It's over now." Oakley glanced at her watch. "I have to go. You coming to the breakfast?" Before hearing Cass's response, off she went in her overdone makeup and hair.

Valinda and Kym approached Cass.

"You two make up?" Valinda asked.

"If you call it that."

After grabbing scrambled eggs, bacon, and coffee from the buffet, the women sat down at one of the eight-person round tables. Oakley tapped the microphone from the podium. Madeline and Ava stood on each side of her. "How is the conference?"

Someone from the back of the room shouted. "Great."

Cass glanced around for Kathryn in hopes of walking to their nine o'clock panel together after breakfast but did not see her.

Oakley continued with conference updates and a reminder that cocktail hour was six to seven and the banquet at seven. She asked authors to come to the podium for a group photo before heading to their panels.

After the photo shoot, Cass walked to her panel and took a seat on the platform. She set her grandmother's romantic, lace embroidered dress from 1930 on the table, along with an antique bracelet. As attendees entered the room, the photographer took an obligatory photo of the panel sans Kathryn who was a no-show. Cass made a note to ask Richard about Kathryn later.

The day consisted of author sessions, lunch, and signings. Cass searched for Richard but did not find him. Since it was time to dress for the banquet, she headed to her room but stopped at the front desk first to leave messages for Richard and Kathryn. She showered and slipped into a burgundy dress that fit like a glove. Win or lose she was ready.

Cocktail hour boomed with authors taking photos and talking. "Richard. I've been looking for you!" Cass approached him.

"Hey there."

"Have you seen Kathryn?"

"Uh…no. Why?"

"She didn't show up for our panel today."

"Is she okay?"

"I'm not sure. Do you have her number?"

"No. You seemed concerned."

"I don't know her very well, but not showing up is concerning."

Valinda and Kym joined them.

"You both look stunning," Cass said. Valinda, dressed in a black cocktail dress and Kym in a maxi dress were all smiles. The three posed for their annual banquet photo, and Cass explained the Kathryn situation.

"I'm sure she's fine," Valinda said. "Let's focus on your nomination tonight."

"They're opening the banquet doors," Kym said.

As a table host, Cass brought copies of her book for the fans at the table. She ordered two bottles of wine, one red and one white.

Madeline stood at the podium asking attendees to take their seats since dinner would be served shortly.

The wait staff closed the ballroom doors.

Dinner consisted of beef, chicken, or vegan, salad, rolls, and a chocolate trifle for dessert. After dinner, a fan asked Cass for another book for her mother. Cass excused herself and quickly went to her room to grab the book. After signing it and exiting her room, a loud thump came from the room across the hall. The door was ajar. Cass hesitated to investigate since the awards would be starting soon. She moved closer and pushed the door open. "Anyone here?"

Cass found Oakley on the floor with a lanyard around her neck. Trembling, Cass knelt down and checked her pulse. She looked closer. Oakley, dressed in a blue taffeta dress and heels, must have been heading to the banquet. To her right lay an empty wine bottle. Had Oakley drunk too much and fallen? How did the lanyard get tangled around her neck?

Thirty minutes later, Cass sat on her bed talking to detective Jax Monroe from the Kill Devil Hills police department. Valinda and Kym sat on the opposite bed, offering moral support. Cass had texted them right after calling the police.

"Let's go over this once more." The detective glanced at his notebook. "You heard a thump as you exited your room then entered Oakley Ray's room to investigate?"

Cass nodded.

"That's when you found her body?"

"Yes."

The detective scratched his head. "What I don't understand is what caused the thump and why did you leave the ceremony to get a book from your room?"

"I don't know what caused the noise, but the book was for a fan at my table."

"What is the fan's name?" The detective gave her a quizzical look.

"I don't remember."

Before responding, an officer entered the room and motioned for the detective to follow him.

"Cass, you okay?" Valinda whispered.

"I'm okay. Just the shock of finding her like that."

"Did you know Oakley's room was near yours?" Kym asked.

"No. I never saw her passing in the hall or anything."

The detective entered the room. "There's a development."

Cass raised her eyebrows.

"Madeline Larue and Ava Ellery gave statements that you and Oakley argued at dinner then again in the bar. Did you have a grudge against Ms. Ray?"

Cass's legs trembled. "We had a disagreement that was cleared up this morning."

"What was the disagreement?"

"I overheard two authors say items on Oakley's panel were fake."

"And who were the authors?"

"I don't know."

"So, you don't know what the noise was in Oakley's room, or the fan's name, or the two women who made the remarks?"

"No."

The detective closed his notebook. "I need you to stay in your room until further notice."

A short while later, Cass packed up her suitcase and conference items. She was ready to head home to Chesapeake. She rubbed her forehead as a knock sounded on her door.

Detective Monroe stood at the door. "May I come in?"

Cass waved her hand in the air.

He sat in the chair by the desk. Cass sat on the bed.

"Looks like you're packed up." He pointed toward the suitcase.

"I want to go home."

"Since the conference doesn't end until tomorrow, I need you to stay."

"Am I a suspect?" Cass started crying.

His voice softened. "I need to cover all bases and need you close by for questions."

"Can I visit my friends?"

"Yes. Just don't leave the hotel." He stood and patted her shoulder. "I'll be back later."

Cass called Valinda and Kym. They returned to her room.

"What happened at the banquet?" Cass asked.

"The minions got up on stage and let attendees know there had been an accident and the awards were canceled," Kym said.

"What did everyone do?"

"Some hung around the ballroom, others moved to the bar. Word on the street was, you used the book as an excuse to leave the banquet and murder Oakley."

"Who said that?"

"The minions."

"But the banquet had started, and Oakley wasn't there."

"I know. Hopefully, the detective will find the murderer," Kym said.

"I have a theory about that," Cass offered.

Valinda and Kym inched toward the edge of the bed.

"When I found her, a bottle of Blushing Blush wine was on the floor. Oakley only drank L'Amour. She told us that herself."

"So?" Kym frowned.

"I'm thinking the killer brought the wine to her room."

"Who?" Valinda asked.

"That I don't know." Cass paused. "Have either of you seen Richard or Kathryn?"

They shook their heads.

"I need to talk to them. Richard was her best friend, and Kathryn hasn't been seen today."

"Is there a connection?" Valinda asked.

"I'm not sure. I'm curious though."

"What are you thinking?"

"I'll sit on a bench in the back of the lobby to see if Richard and Kathryn pass by. The detective said I could leave my room but not to leave the hotel."

"Are you up to seeing the other authors?" Kym asked.

"No," Cass said.

Valinda stood. "I've got you covered. "I always travel with wigs. You can use a black one that I brought. It'll make a great disguise."

After fitting Cass's blond curls into the wig, she stared at her image in the mirror. She wondered if her family would recognize her.

The three women sat in the back of the lobby and watched the comings and goings.

"There's Richard," Valinda pointed out. "I'll get him."

As Richard and Valinda walked to the bench, he gave Cass a curious look.

"It's me. Cass."

"What's with the getup?"

"I'm undercover."

"For what?"

"I'm trying to find out who killed Oakley. Have you seen Kathryn?"

"No. Why?"

"When I found Oakley, a bottle of wine was by her. The wine was not her brand."

"What does that have to do with her murder?"

"I don't know, but I need your help. See if you can find Kathryn and bring her over."

Richard approached the bench a short while later.

"No luck?" Cass asked.

He shook his head. "I'll keep looking. What is your room number?"

"Two twenty-two."

He disappeared into the bar.

It was midnight and the women were tired.

"I'm ready for bed." Valinda yawned.

"Me too." Kym stretched her arms.

"You both go to bed. I'll text if something comes up."

As the night continued, a few authors remained. Since Richard had not returned, Cass approached the front desk.

"May I help you?" the clerk asked.

Cass left a message for Kathryn to come to her room as soon as possible.

"Anything else?"

"I need an extra room key."

After the clerk gave her a key, Cass entered the bar and sat on the far end.

Matt approached her. "What cha' having?"

"A glass of Blushing Blush."

"Coming right up." He set the wine before her. "That's our newest wine on tap. We have bottles to go, if interested."

"Oh really?"

"Yeah. A man ordered a bottle for a toast, and then a woman ordered a bottle to go."

"Interesting." Cass took a sip.

"Are you with the writers' conference?"

Matt didn't recognize her in the black wig. "Yes. I'm staying in the hotel."

"Gotcha." He paused. "How's the wine?"

"Cool and light. I'll take a bottle."

"We're closing shortly." He lowered his voice. "I can bring a bottle to your room."

Smooth. "Uh…that sounds great."

"What's your room number?"

Cass slipped him the extra key. "Two twenty-two." Matt put the wine on her tab, and she said goodbye.

On the ride up in the elevator, she texted Valinda and Kym to come to her room since Matt was on his way. Could he have been the one who killed Oakley? As she opened her room door, someone shoved her from behind.

Cass turned and faced Richard. Her heart raced.

"I knew you were getting close." He shut the door.

"What do you mean?"

"When you told me the wine bottle was not Oakley's, I knew you would figure it out. The bottle in Oakley's room was mine."

"You're a Scotch drinker."

"True. I also drink Blushing Blush. You saw me drink it at dinner."

Cass remembered Richard drinking the wine and realized he was the man that Matt said ordered the bottle for a toast. "You killed Oakley. Why?"

"Each year before the banquet, Oak and I would toast in her room. This year, I brought Blushing Blush and she hated it. Said I was inconsiderate. She wouldn't stop. When she put her lanyard on, I strangled her. I don't know what got into me."

Cass looked toward the door for an escape.

"And now that you know I killed her, I have to kill you." Richard grabbed her neck.

She struggled to breath. If she didn't do something, he would kill her. She reached for her lanyard on the bed and lassoed it around his neck.

He loosened his grip.

She tightened hers.

"Ouch. You bitch."

Cass ran toward the door. Richard grabbed her leg and yanked her to the floor. He jumped on her back.

She punched his groin.

He rolled off and curled up on the floor.

Just as she started for the door, it opened. Matt entered with a wine bottle. "What the hell?"

Valinda and Kym ran in behind him.

Richard tried to make a run for it.

"Richard killed Oakley," Cass yelled.

Matt tripped Richard.

Richard fell into the hallway at Kathryn's feet.

Cass ran to the door. "Kathryn, what are you doing here?"

"I got your messages from the front desk."

Detective Monroe raced down the hallway. "Stop that man."

"What are you doing?" Cass asked the detective.

"Richard killed Oakley. We got him on security video."

The next morning, Cass met Valinda and Kym at checkout.

While standing in the lobby, Cass saw Madeline and Ava approaching.

"Since the votes were already cast, you won Best Historical Novel," Madeline said. "The award will be mailed to you even though we don't agree with it." The two women stormed off.

The win was bittersweet. Before Cass could react, Kathryn rolled her luggage toward her.

"Congrats on your award," Kathryn said. "I saw Madeline at the coffee stand."

"Thanks. I'm sorry you couldn't make the panel. Is everything okay?"

"About that. I was with Matt. He offered room service and tried to blackmail me." Tears streamed down her face.

"I'm sorry." Cass said.

Kathryn wiped her tears. "The thing is, I liked him." She sniffed. "I let hotel security and the conference coordinators know, and Matt was fired."

"You did the right thing," Cass suggested. "Hope to see you next year." She waved goodbye to Kathryn.

The valet brought the women's cars to the front of the hotel. Cass, Valinda, and Kym made plans to meet soon. As Cass shut her trunk, Detective Monroe stood on the side.

"Taking off?" he asked.

"Uh…yeah." She frowned.

"Since Richard confessed, I don't have any further questions."

"Okay." Cass walked to the driver's side.

He followed.

"If you're ever in the Outer Banks, look me up." He extended his card to her.

Cass hesitated.

"This is personal, not police business." He smiled. "My cell number is on the card."

Cass took the card. She reached into her bag and grabbed a card. "If you're in Chesapeake, look me up."

GRAPE MINDS DRINK ALIKE
by Allie Marie

Gordon Burrell pushed through the interior foyer doors leading to the pizzeria, the knuckles of his right hand white from his death-grip on the briefcase he carried. He blinked until his eyes adjusted to the dim light of the room, his gaze first falling on the lone diner before locking on the bartender drying glasses.

The beefy man at the table tilted his head toward an empty seat across from him and Gordon strode toward the table.

Neither man shook hands, but merely nodded. Gordon set the briefcase flat on the chair to the right of the diner, then settled in the designated seat.

"It's all there?" Starkey Lombardo asked, peering at the case through narrowed eyes.

"All there—a cool quarter mil."

"Where's the dame?"

"Running late. She'll just join us for a celebratory bottle of wine. There's an envelope under the—stuffing—that has all the details, in case you have to leave before she arrives. She wants it done tonight."

"Hubby must have pissed her off big time."

Gordon shrugged and reached for a menu. "I've never met him. Most of the dough in that case is mine. She'll pay me back after his insurance pays off. You got the necklace?"

Starkey casually flipped the locks on the briefcase, tilted the top and poked around. Nodding in satisfaction, he snapped the lid shut and pushed the locks in place. He reached inside his suit coat and withdrew a slim blue velvet box, opening it to reveal a strand of diamonds with a large teardrop at the center.

Gordon took the jewel case and twitched the box under the lights. With each move, the facets of the diamonds glistened one way, sparkled the next. "Perfect."

"Well, everything's in place. It'll all be done before midnight tonight."

"The less I know the better." Both men perused their menus and decided on spaghetti dinners. Starkey snapped his fingers.

The man behind the bar picked up a pad. Dressed as if he was an extra on the set of *The Godfather*, he wore a white shirt with black bow tie, black slacks, and an apron tucked into his waistband. As he crossed the room to take their order, he pulled a pen from his shirt pocket.

Starkey ordered salads, breadsticks, and two spaghetti and meatball platters.

"Put it all on my tab," he called to the silent waiter's departing back. "I just got paid tonight." His flabby jowls flapped as his roar of laughter echoed around the room.

"He doesn't say much, does he?" Gordon jutted his chin toward the departing waiter.

"Salvatore? Nope. That's why I like this place. You can count on discretion. Listen, I've got another—client—coming by to—er, make a payment. I don't usually mix two business deals at the same time, but he's in as much of a hurry as you and your dame are. He wants his wife outta the picture and fast. Hope you don't mind."

"Naw, as long as I don't have to know the deets."

Starkey snapped his fingers at the waiter. "Music, Salvatore."

Still without uttering a word, the server walked down the length of the bar area and turned toward a stereo on a shelf. Seconds later, music from an Italian operetta wafted around the room.

Their business deal complete, Starkey called for more wine. The two diners polished off their meals in silence.

Salvatore came over to remove the empty plates just as the double doors swung open and a well-dressed man carrying a briefcase stepped through. Much as Gordon had done earlier, he blinked as he glanced around the room before settling his gaze on the occupants of the table. He hesitated, a scowl lining his face.

Starkey stood and called him over. "All's good, Sinclair. Come on over."

The newcomer strolled over, his glare raking Gordon. Nearly mirroring the latter's previous actions, Sinclair set a cognac-colored *Bruno Cucinelli* leather portfolio in the empty seat beside the beefy Starkey, then sat opposite Gordon.

"No intros, no names," he demanded.

"Fine. Where's your wife?" Starkey checked the contents of the pouch, closed it with a satisfied nod and set it beside the other.

Sinclair rolled his eyes toward the ceiling. "You know women. She had to stop at the powder room 'to freshen up.' That'll take a half hour. The woman spends thousands on salons and makeup, but she still has to 'freshen up' every time she passes a mirror." He pulled a wineglass from the place setting to his left and drew it in front of him. At the same time, Gordon moved his empty glass toward the bottle.

"Great minds and all that shit." Starkey poured the merlot. The trio raised their glasses in toast and drained their wine.

"Turn the volume up on the TV," Starkey demanded, snapping his finger toward the bar. "This place is like a morgue and my favorite movie is on."

The diners and the waiter turned toward the overhead television, where a muted *The Godfather* played, the flickering blue light casting an eerie glow over the bar area. Salvatore grabbed the remote and turned up the volume just at the scene where the toll-taker dropped down in his booth and Sonny met his fate in a hail of gunfire.

"My favorite part." Starkey's laughter turned into a wheeze. He snapped his fingers at the waiter again and motioned toward the newcomer.

"I'd be pissed if you did that to me all the time," Gordon said, snapping his fingers.

Starkey shrugged. Salvatore brought a menu to Sinclair, who shook his head. The waiter then cleared the meal dishes away.

When he returned, he brought fresh glasses and a new bottle of chianti.

"Compliments of the house," the man of few words said. He filled the clean glasses with chianti and then took the last of the dinner plates away.

Starkey swirled and sniffed the wine. "Top-notch grapes." After another toast, the men drank in silence.

"Turn on the a/c, Salvatore!" Starkey shouted as he loosened the tie at his collar. He set down his glass with less than a third of wine left. He didn't believe in baby sips.

Salvatore straightened and clicked another remote, his elbow knocking over a tray, sending glasses crashing to the floor.

At that moment, the restaurant doors pushed open. A stacked blonde in a form-fitting red dress walked through, her high heels pecking across the wooden floor.

Gordon stood. Both he and Sinclair said in unison, "Andrea," then turned shocked faces toward each other.

"What the...?" Gordon began.

"Hiya, babe," Starkey said.

Both men turned to Starkey, who held a black Colt 1911 aimed right a Gordon's chest.

Salvatore stood a few feet away, pointing a Glock 19 at Sinclair. Silencers adorned the barrels of both weapons.

"Sit down. Both of you." Starkey waved the gun in the direction of the seats.

Both men dropped to their chairs, stunned looks etched on their faces.

Andrea continued her sashay to the table, bypassing both her husband and her lover as they glared at her. Taking a stance behind Starkey, the willowy blonde wrapped her arms around his neck and pressed her cheek to his sweating face, her gaze flicking between the two dumbfounded men.

"Hello, boys," she said with a sardonic smile. She lifted the linen napkin from around Starkey's neck and patted his perspiring face. "Hello, poopsie."

"Hello, sweetie." Starkey jerked his disheveled tie free and threw it to the floor, then loosened his top three buttons.

Beads of sweat glistened off the foreheads of all three men seated at the table. Gordon clutched his temples and leaned to his right, retching violently. A moment later, he collapsed into a quivering mass in the puddle of puke.

Sinclair's face grew ashy before he too toppled from his chair, convulsing with even more violent seizures. Bloody bile spewed from his mouth as his head lolled from side to side.

Starkey snickered as he reached for his glass. Salvatore moved into the older man's view as Andrea moved to stand beside the waiter. The two embraced and engaged in a passionate kiss.

"What the hell are you doing?" Starkey tried to stand but doubled over, his chin glistening with drool.

She broke from the kiss to cast a sidelong glance and said, "You're bigger and beefier than those two. It'll take longer. But don't worry, it's coming! Potassium cyanide may not be painless, but it's fast. And less messy than a bullet to the brain." She looked at the disheveled bodies of the other two men, then added with a giggle, "Well, sort of."

"You bitch!" Starkey struggled to his feet, his eyes bulging wide. His upper body lifted with ragged gasps as he struggled to catch his breath. He clutched his chest and keeled over backwards, pulling the tablecloth with him. Bottles and glassware shattered around him.

Andrea and Salvatore went back to their lip lock.

Finally, the waiter broke the embrace. "Did you shut down the lights and turn off the 'Open' sign when you came in?"

"I did, and posted the 'Vacationing in Italy. See you in three weeks' sign on the door. I locked interior and exterior doors too." She pressed her body against his. "Kiss me, Sal."

"Time for that later." He stiffened his arms to move her away and nodded toward the two briefcases. "There's more work to do."

Disregarding the carnage at their feet, each grabbed one valise and carried it to another table, where they gleefully rustled through the packets of money. Then they closed the lids.

Salvatore walked back to the table of doom and pulled the jewel case out from the debris. He faced Andrea and opened it for her.

Her eyes bulged at the jewels.

He nodded. "To celebrate our success tonight—a special gift for you. Turn around and watch in the mirror as I place them on you," he whispered seductively as he removed them from the case.

"Just like in the movies." She giggled and turned her back to him, lifting her hair to expose her neck. Their gaze met in the smoky glass.

He kept his gaze locked with hers as he rained kisses along her nape, then he fastened the diamond strand in place.

"They're so beautiful," she gushed. She turned to throw her arms around the waiter, but he shook his head.

"Not yet. Let me see how stunning you are."

She twirled and stopped in front of him. "You like what you see?"

He tilted his head as he admired her. "Yes, beautiful." He ran the edge of the velvet case along her jaw, across the smaller stones until he stopped at the larger teardrop at the base. The sparkling bauble rested just above her cleavage.

"I had these made just for you, to celebrate tonight. Cost a small fortune, but worth every penny." He looked in her eyes and smiled, then shoved the edge of the box at the pendant. The glass gave way and fluid trickled between her breasts.

"They're fake? Fake diamonds? What..." She looked down, coughing wildly, then back at him. Her eyes flickered in fear as realization struck her. "Salvatore, what did you do? I thought we had it all worked out—to run off to South America and..."

He looked back at the three men slumped around the table.

"Because of you, your sap husband, your lover boy, and poor old lovesick Starkey are all dead. You think I want to be your fourth? As I said, the necklace was specially made just for you."

"But I loved *you.*" Beads of perspiration formed on her trembling upper lip. Violent spasms racked her body and she retched dry heaves before spitting grits.

"What was that you said?" Salvatore asked. "'Potassium cyanide may not be painless but it's fast?' At one hundred pounds, you'll succumb to the effects of it much faster than the men."

While she crumbled into a writhing heap on the floor, he dumped all the money into a larger suitcase he pulled from behind the bar. He stepped over her now-unmoving body and headed toward the kitchen door.

He left the television running. *The Godfather* would loop forever...or at least until someone came to the place.

In three weeks.

He made a quick phone call from his cell. "Is the jet ready, doll?"

A sultry voice answered, "Yes. So am I."

"Have them fire the engines. I'll be at the airport in ten and we'll be on our way to Costa Rica."

"My engine will be running too. Bye, lover," the female cooed.

He turned his phone off, took a last look around him, and headed toward the rear door of the restaurant.

As if on second thought, he did an about-face and stepped back to the table. He snapped his fingers in Starkey's direction, and *then* continued to make his exodus.

REVENGE ON THE ROCKS
by Betsy Ashton

The last time Maddie heard from her twin Millie was a series of text messages. The woman who couldn't go twelve hours without checking in had been silent for an entire day. Maddie reread the messages she'd already read fifty times.

One month earlier. **HI, SIS, IT'S ME. JUST GOT AN INTERESTING HIT ON LETSMEET.COM. I RESPONDED.**

Three days later. **ME AGAIN. DECIDED TO MEET HIM. WE HAD COFFEE AND TALKED FOR ABOUT AN HOUR.**

One week later. **MILLIE, HERE. MEETING BRAD THIS AFTERNOON. HE'S REALLY CUTE.**

NOT QUITE TDH—*Wait, what?* Maddie thought for a minute. *Of course, tall, dark, and handsome*--**BUT CLOSE. OLDER THAN HE WROTE IN HIS PROFILE, BUT, HEY, EVERYBODY LIES ON THESE SITES. WE'RE GOING FOR A WALK IN THE PARK.**

One week later. **I'M SO EXCITED. BRAD'S REALLY THOUGHTFUL. BROUGHT ME A BOOK WE TALKED ABOUT. WE'RE GOING TO A MOVIE TONIGHT.**

One day before. **FINALLY, WE'RE GOING TO DINNER. HIS FAVORITE DRINK IS A BLACK RUSSIAN. I LOVE WHITE RUSSIANS, SO WE HAVE ONE MORE THING IN COMMON. BTW, I NEVER PUT MY FAVORITE DRINK IN MY PROFILE, SO DON'T WORRY. I'LL CALL OR TEXT WHEN I GET HOME. WISH ME LUCK. ILY.**

Maddie drove to her sister's apartment. *Where is she? Is she all right?* She let herself in and did a quick walk through the rooms. Typical of her sister. *Not like my place. Well, fraternal twins aren't supposed to behave exactly the same way.* Not an item out of place, except for a discarded dress folded on the bed. *She must have changed her mind about what to wear. She must really like this guy.*

Maddie looked for her sister's phone and handbag. Not there, so she hadn't returned after her date with TDH. Her laptop was on her desk. Maddie stuffed it into her tote. She looked for anything else that might identify where Millie had gone or who she was with. Nothing.

A small meow from the bathroom lured Maddie through the bedroom. A black-and-white tuxedo kitten bounced out and rubbed against her legs. She peeked into the bath. Nearly empty bowls for food and water. *Millie had planned to come home.* The litter pan needed scooping.

"Well, Shamu, where's your mommy?"

"Meow."

"You're no help at all. Do you think your mommy would go off and not leave extra food?" Maddie scratched the kitten's ears before searching for her carrier. She set it on the floor and watched her walk in and curl up. "Guess you're going home with me until Millie returns."

Maddie latched the carrier, hoisted the tote onto her shoulder, and locked the front door. She stopped at the pet store for supplies. Her brow furrowed; her brain churned.

Where the hell is she? Is she with TDH? Maddie sucked in a deep breath. *Something's wrong. I don't know what, but she'd never leave without a trace. Especially not without the kitten.*

Once home with Shamu curled up beside her on the couch and Millie's laptop open, she scrolled through her social media accounts and emails for any clue to Millie's whereabouts. And who she might be with. Facebook, Twitter, Instagram, Pinterest. Nothing. Any social media account for a mention of either Millie or Brad, a.k.a., TDH. Millie was prominent online, but this Brad fellow wasn't. Or if he was, it was under a different name. And not a single picture of Millie with him.

Maddie tried several dating websites but couldn't get very far without having to set up—and pay for—a subscription.

That shit isn't going to happen.

She fed the kitten before settling down to pick at a sandwich. Before long, and after a visit to her new litter pan, Shamu hopped into Maddie's lap, turned around twice, and curled up in a ball, purring so loudly Maddie had to laugh. "I hope you don't do that all night, or I won't get a wink of sleep."

Television held no allure. Programs came and went; commercials shouted at her to buy something she didn't want. The late news covered local events but nothing about a missing woman, her sister, her best friend. Maddie reached for a pad and pen to make a list of things to do the next day. Top of the list was the police. She hadn't covered the cop beat for her local paper for years not to know they wouldn't do anything until at least twenty-four hours had passed. And then, only if it had been a quiet night, crime wise. Well, twenty-four hours *had* passed. She didn't give a damn about how busy the cops were. Her sister was missing.

Maddie's trip to the downtown police station was fraught with irony. The desk sergeant told her to "fill out this form."

She did.

The sergeant tossed it into an inbox and tried to dismiss her. She remained planted in front of his counter, feet apart, hands on hips, restating her desire to speak to a detective. The sergeant was equally adamant. She'd filed the proper form. He was done with her.

"What's going on here, sergeant?" a voice came from behind Maddie's left hip. She turned to see a familiar face. Fred Galbraith, a former homicide detective retired on disability and Millie's former boyfriend, wheeled forward. Maddie leaned over and kissed his cheek.

"How did you know it was me?"

"Get real. That stance, that no-nonsense voice. I knew the minute I came into the room. Now, tell me what's going on." Fred led the way to an empty interview room. "I hadn't heard you'd returned to covering the PD."

"I haven't." In a few rapid sentences, Maddie outlined her fears for her sister. "I know she's either been kidnapped. Or worse."

"Settle down. Why did you jump to these conclusions? Did she say anything?"

Maddie fished her phone out of her tote, swiped to Millie's texts, and handed the device over. Fred scrolled through the entries.

"Is this all?"

"Well, yeah. You know Millie. She's the text and tweet queen. Nothing since Saturday night. It's not like her."

"I'll grant you that. Who's this Brad guy? And what the hell does TDH mean? Some new text acronym I don't use?" Fred returned the phone.

"Old school. Tall, dark and handsome."

"Well. What would I know? Definitely not my description." He ran his hands through thinning red hair and shifted his gaunt frame in the wheelchair. "Could she have fallen for this guy and gone off on a long weekend without telling you?"

"I hardly think so. Millie may live out loud on social media, but she's ultra-conservative in how and where she meets guys. I don't think she's ever had a casual hook up."

Maddie watched the flow of officers around the squad room. "I can't believe she'd leave on her own accord without letting me know. And she would NEVER leave Shamu without food or water."

"What's a Shamu?"

"Her new kitten. She's at my apartment."

"Let me rattle a cage or two. Maybe I can find something, maybe not. You filed a missing person's report?"

"Just before you came in." She leaned against the wall.

"Go home. If Millie's all right, she'll call you."

Maddie nodded. "I can't just sit around doing nothing. And I have no idea what to tell our parents."

"Yes, you can. And you must." Fred rolled to the door to usher her out. "Don't call your folks for a day or two. And for God's sake, don't do anything rash."

Maddie shook her head. "When have I ever done anything rash?"

"I don't have time to count. Now, lean over and give me a kiss." Maddie did as ordered.

"I'll call you soon."

*

With so many false starts over the past month, Maddie no longer lurched for the phone when she heard Fred's ring tone. She struggled to maintain hope. Not hope that Millie was alive but that the police would locate her body. When the phone rang at five in the morning, Maddie rolled over and answered.

"Hello?" Voice thick with sleep and despair, Maddie knew this would be bad news.

"Maddie?" Fred asked.

"Who else would answer my phone?"

"Don't grouch at me." Fred took a deep breath. "Police got a tip three hours ago. I think they found Millie's body."

Maddie gasped. She closed her eyes before asking, "Her body? Where is it?"

"Right now, in a shallow grave. The detectives on the scene say it looks like it's been there a while. The crime scene team's there but can't get started until it's light."

"Where is it?" Maddie threw off the covers. Her naked body broke out in overall goose flesh when the chilled bedroom air hit her blanket-warmed skin. "Tell me."

"No. You can't rush to the scene. You know better." Fred kept his cop-voice steady. "You'll do Millie no good if you do."

"Tell me, dammit." She hunted for jeans and a sweatshirt.

"No. Listen to me. Millie was buried. That's about all we know. That means she didn't die of natural causes, or, if she did, whoever she was with panicked. Let the police and the crime scene guys do their job. Once Millie's at the medical examiner's office, I'll take you there." Fred swore. Horns blared in the background. And outside Maddie's front door.

"Where are you? Sounds like you're close by."

"Getting out of my car in front of your apartment building. You don't want to be alone."

Maddie rushed to the buzzer to release the downstairs lock. She paced until she heard the elevator stop on her floor. By the time she unlocked and opened the door, Fred was rolling himself toward her. She threw herself into his arms, nearly tangling her feet in his wheels.

"Let's get back inside. We don't want to wake the building."

Maddie led the way into the kitchen where she put on a pot of coffee. Her hands trembled so much she spilled grounds on the countertop and floor.

"Come here." Fred maneuvered into the small kitchen. He pulled Maddie down and held her.

Maddie sobbed on his shoulder. Shamu woke up, stretched, and leaped into her lap. He tapped her cheek with one white paw.

"I'm here. We'll find out what happened. I promise."

"I prayed for a different outcome."

"Me, too. Millie and I may have broken up before my accident, but I never stopped loving her. Or you."

*

Over the next few hours, they drank pots of coffee. Maddie paced; Fred worked his phone for information. Just before dinnertime, he had the news he needed.

"Okay." Fred took a deep breath. "Here's what we know. A jogger found a red-haired woman's body in a shallow grave in Wordsworth Park. His dog alerted him. The jogger called 9-1-1 and waited at the scene. Officers, detectives, and crime scene investigators worked all day on recovery. They cleared the jogger. The spot's pretty isolated, so canvassing the area to interview people would be fruitless."

"Where's her body?" Maddie sucked in a deep breath, tightening her stomach muscles at the same time.

"At the M.E.'s office. They're not sure, but they think it's Millie."

"Why not? Surely, they could tell."

"The body's been in the ground long enough for decomposition to begin. They bagged and tagged her clothing, what there was of it. I hope you can make a positive identification."

"I want to see her." Maddie grabbed her handbag and headed for the door.

Fred snagged her arm before she took more than one step. "No. You. Don't. You want to remember the Millie you loved, I loved, not what was done to her. Let the police deal with that."

Maddie fought Fred, but his grip only tightened. "Let me go."

"NO! Listen to me. I'll drive you to the M.E.'s office to look at her clothing. Please don't ask to see her." Fred led the way to the elevator.

*

Maddie handed her identification to the M.E. "I'm Madelaine Rodgers. You have my sister's body here. Millicent Nokes."

"Fred, did you tell her what we need?"

"I did. She's not to see the body. She's here to identify personal belongings." Fred gripped Maddie's hand.

"Wait in here." The M.E. disappeared through a locked door. Moments later, she reappeared with several sealed bags, which she set on a stainless-steel examination table.

Maddie gulped, picked up each bag, and scrutinized it. Tears welled but didn't fall. "I gave my sister this sweater for Christmas last year. It was her favorite. The slacks could be hers. She had several pairs of black ones. The shoes, I don't recognize. Millie was a clothes horse, so they're probably hers."

"Was she raped?" Fred asked the question Maddie couldn't.

"Not that we can tell. We won't know if she was incapacitated until we get the tox screen back."

Two bags remained: Millie's small date purse and the few items she carried with her. "I don't see her driver's license or money. She'd never leave home without them."

Fred took the bag with the loose contents. "No phone?"

The M.E. shook her head. "It wasn't with the bagged items.

Maybe the police kept it. All I have is what you see."

"No house keys," Maddie said. "Oh, shit. I have to tell the super to change the locks."

"Let's ask the detectives, first. Maybe they have keys and phone."

Maddie nodded. "From this, I think it's my sister. I can be positive if I see her."

"Not going to happen, Maddie," Fred said. "I warned you…"

Maddie ignored him. "My sister has a small, red birthmark just below her right collarbone. About the size of a dime. Rough edges. We called it her 'vicious circle.'"

"Crap. I forgot about that." Fred released Maddie's hand before turning to the M.E. "Can you check?"

"A vicious circle? Apt description. It's there. We can positively identify the cor—, um, body. Thanks for coming down. If we need anything more, I'll be in touch. I'm really sorry for your loss, Ms. Rodgers."

*

Fred drove in silence back to Maddie's apartment.

"Who the hell murdered her?" Maddie's anger erupted in a fit of fury. She walked around her living room, fists flailing, unable to sit. She wanted revenge on the killer. And she wanted it now.

"The police are searching for clues. If they found anything, they haven't released the information."

"Where do we go from here?"

"I'm not sure. I want to find TDH, a.k.a. Brad. I asked my buddies in records to search for him, but with only a single first name, no description, and no last name, they laughed." Fred ran his hands through his hair, leaving it spiked.

"I've searched social media for any picture of Millie with any guy." Maddie grimaced. "Why did she have to be so damned private?"

Fred laughed. "I agree. Millie never took selfies."

"If we find her phone, I bet we find at least one pic of TDH. Probably a candid he didn't know about." Maddie scrolled through screen after screen on Millie's laptop, something she'd done a thousand times. "What if we're going about this all wrong? What if we need to set a trap?"

"I don't like where you're going. Don't do anything. I'll be right back." He rolled away from the kitchen table, which had become their shared workspace, and down the hall to the bathroom.

"You're not thinking about putting yourself out there to trap 'Brad.' Are you?" He asked when he returned.

"What other option do we have?"

"I don't like it."

"Look, I tried hacking into Millie's LetsMeet account. I tried every possible password until I got locked out."

"Did you ask for a password reset?"

Maddie glared. "Of course, I did. Nothing. She didn't use any word I knew for her recovery term."

"Okay. What are you thinking?" He handed her a ham sandwich. Meals had been haphazard since Millie's death. Fred had taken over seeing they ate.

"I'm thinking about starting a LetsMeet account for me. Maybe 'Brad' will bite."

"I don't like it."

"You already said that. What other options do we have except waiting to see if another body turns up? And you know how much I love to sit around doing nothing."

Fred laughed before taking a huge bite. "You have never been the wait-and-see type."

"Not when it's my sister who's waiting for revenge."

"Millie isn't waiting for revenge. You are."

"Whatever."

They finished lunch in silence.

Maddie watched the kitten chase a red dot across the living room floor. Ever since Fred brought the laser over, Shamu got lots of exercise. "Time to write up my profile. What should I use as a photo?"

"Go fix your hair like Millie's. I'll take a couple of pictures."

"Good idea. Millie and I are fraternal twins, my hair is brown. She was red, but we should be able to get close enough to tempt him. I hope."

Hours later, Maddie, a.k.a. Liz Webber, was live on LetsMeet.

*

A month after posting Liz's profile, Maddie got a credible bite. The guy said he loved walking in parks, long chats over coffee, and reading. He offered a sample of his then-current reading list: Chaucer, Shakespeare, and Stephen King.

"Totally trying to cover all bases, don'tcha think?" Maddie laughed. "He's lying. I doubt anyone on LetsMeet reads the classics. Maybe most don't read at all."

"Aren't you being cynical? I do agree about the classics. I just don't want to damn all who are 'looking for love in all the wrong places' by saying they don't read. After all, he read your profile. So, tell me about this dude."

"He suggested getting together. His profile says his name is 'Paul.'"

Fred and Maddie wrote a response. Liz also loved walking in parks, which her profile clearly said. She didn't mention reading either in her profile or in her response. Neither did she offer to meet.

A day later, Paul responded with an invitation for coffee. He named a small shop, not Starbucks, but an indie on the outskirts of the city. She turned him down. Too far out of town.

"I work, so a smaller shop in the city is better."

Three weeks passed.

"Did we scare him off?" Maddie wondered. "Was I playing too hard to catch?"

"I don't think so. Let's post a picture of you sitting in Wordsworth Park next to that famous statue. See if he bites."

He did. He, too, loved Wordsworth. The statue was powerful, mesmerizing. Could they buy their own coffee and meet there?

"I'll say yes."

Fred watched Maddie fix her hair like her sister's once again. He had arranged for one of his off-duty detective buddies to watch the rendezvous and take pictures. What he sent were clear, unobstructed pictures of a handsome man, too perfectly groomed.

"A real charmer," Fred muttered. He waited until Maddie returned to get her take.

"It's him. He made a couple of mistakes. Said I reminded him of someone he'd met and grown fond of... I had difficulty not calling him out on the spot."

"I'll bet."

"The more he talked, the more I was sure he was the guy Millie met. When he mentioned black Russians as his favorite drink, a detail not in Paul/Brad's profile, I had a chance to tell him how much I loved white Russians. He flinched."

"We should go to the police."

"With what? A suspicion that a guy I met on a dating site murdered my sister?"

"They wouldn't take us seriously."

"I'm going to get even. And I won't tell you because it won't be legal. You're still a cop at heart."

"Just be careful."

*

Maddie called a source she'd used when writing a series of articles on getting away with murder using untraceable poisons. She slipped out to a small shop several miles away from both her office and her home to buy a prepaid phone. She sat on a bench in a nondescript pocket park and called Dr. Regina McNamara, such a leading poison expert her nickname was "the poison lady."

51

"Gina? It's Maddie Rodgers. How are you?"

"Maddie? I haven't talked to you in ages. Are you working on a new exposé for the paper?" Gina's husky voice attested to years of smoking. "How can I help?"

Maddie told Gina she needed poisons that were easy to acquire, lethal but not immediately so, and tasteless.

"Hell, girl, you don't ask for much, do you?" Gina laughed before descending into a coughing fit. When she caught her breath, she offered a couple of suggestions. "My first thought is strychnine. Easy to administer. Orally, as a dust, even injected. But if used orally, it has a distinctive bitter almond taste. Not be the best for your exposé."

"What else?"

"There are hundreds of poisons from fast- to slow-acting like fentanyl. Fancy poisons like Russia's favorites, polonium and Novichok. Or North Korea's nerve agent, VX."

"And where the hell would I get them and not leave a trail?"

"Oh, you are cranky, aren't you? No trail, huh?" Gina paused. Maddie heard a hand slap a hard surface. "Oh, hell. Forget the exotics. Go to the drugstore and buy a bottle of eye drops."

"Eye drops?"

"Yes. Empty a bottle in a drink to cause death, although not immediately. Rapid heartbeat, blurred vision, drowsiness, convulsions." Gina paused. "I'd go with eye drops."

"Thanks, Gina. We didn't have this conversation." Maddie warned.

"Of course not. How many times have you called with questions about poisons?"

"Too many to count."

"But never from a burner phone." Gina laughed.

"Right. Never from a burner. Speak with you later."

*

Maddie, a.k.a., Liz, set up a dinner date with Paul/Brad/whomever at a bistro several miles from her apartment. She fussed with her hair and makeup. She even wore the dress Millie had discarded. *For luck.* She arrived to find him already seated with a drink on the table.

"So nice to see you. I'm glad we are together." Paul stood and kissed her on the cheek.

"Me, too." She allowed hm to pull out her chair. The waiter appeared as soon as she was settled.

"What are you drinking, Paul?"

"A black Russian."

"I'll have my favorite."

"One white Russian," Paul ordered.

Maddie placed her small handbag on her lap under the table. She fiddled with the clasp until she was sure she could easily open it to reach the eye drops inside.

Paul raised a toast. "I've only met one other woman who drank white Russians. To us."

"To her." Maddie's voice was cold.

Paul took a hearty slug and encouraged Liz/Maddie to do the same. She sipped. When he was on his second drink, and she still on her first, she excused herself to go to the restroom. She leaned over and kissed him, letting him kiss her more deeply than she wanted. She distracted him long enough to empty a bottle of eye drops into his drink.

"I'll be right back," she whispered. She glanced back before entering the women's room to see Paul drop something into her drink. *He's trying to roofie me. Just like he did Millie. And just like I did with his drink.*

She returned to her seat in time to watch Paul finish his second drink and raise a finger for another round. His expression changed; he yawned and shook his head.

"These never hit me hard. Must need to eat." His speech slurred.

Maddie leaned in, pretending to be concerned. "I'm not the first woman you roofied who drank white Russians." Low and ominous, Maddie delivered the *coup de grâce*.

"Huh?"

"You spiked my twin sister's drink half a year ago. A redhead named Millie."

"Who?"

"My sister, asshole. Just before you killed her. Why did you do it, Brad?"

"Brad?" Paul shook his head. "I need some air."

"Let me help you." She threw money on the table before steering a now-reeling drunk out of the bar.

"My car's over here," Paul said.

Maddie leaned in as he tried and failed to buckle his seatbelt. "This is for my sister Millie. Karma's a bitch, isn't she? You never know when she's going to show up and bite you in the ass."

Maddie slammed the door and watched Paul pull away from the curb. She walked to her own car and entered the traffic flow a few lengths behind Paul. He sped up and slowed down, swung from one lane to another.

Jeez, please don't let him kill another innocent person.

Cars scattered like drops of mercury on a tabletop. Maddie pushed into a hole in the traffic right behind Paul's car. She watched him slump forward. The horn blared. He sped up one last time before swerving into a bridge stanchion at full speed. Police sirens screamed behind her. Maddie drove past just as the gas tank exploded, raised a finger in the air, and smiled.

"Revenge on the rocks is so sweet, you bastard."

SWIPING RIGHT
by Kristin Kisska

The dive bar's orange neon sign sizzles as I pass under to tug open the sticky door. Inside the old Hitch & Swig, hollow country tunes wail from a jukebox. Few people populate the near-empty tavern. A lone waitress hustles longneck beers on her scuffed plastic tray.

As I venture toward the bar, a slouching patron glances up from his drink, eyeballs my sundress and sandals, then loses interest. The wafting scent of stale beer envelops me, leaving a residue on my skin. A break at the pool table sends balls scattering into worn pockets. My arms sprout goosebumps despite the muggy night air.

Crap. He's late.

"Can I get you a drink?" The bartender, who looks old and tired enough to be an original employee, wipes the warped bartop as I approach, then places a cocktail napkin in front of me.

"Two tequila shots, please."

As he leaves to fill my order, I use my reflection in the dingy mirror behind the bar to touch up my lip gloss. I should've suggested someplace nicer. Safer. Something with fewer mosquitos. Opening my phone's app, I glance at the profile of my blind date one last time.

Moments later, my pulse picks up its tempo when the front door slams shut and a blond, middle-aged man approaches the bar. It's him. Thank God.

"Corynne?" He plops down on the barstool next to mine and faces me. "I'd recognize you anywhere. You look exactly like your profile picture."

"Nice to meet you, Tad." I try to keep my cool and not look too excited, but adrenalin pumps through my veins. "I'm glad you swiped right."

"For a pretty lady like you? Of course!" While he still sports a chiseled jaw and full head of hair, his picture had to have been either airbrushed or taken a few too many years ago. That's okay. Both of our profile pictures were doctored. "Besides, I have a thing for long blond hair."

I'd been counting on that. Every picture posted on Tad's Instagram page is with some leggy blond or another. I reach for my shot glass. "I ordered for both of us. Tequila?"

"Sure. Let's get this party started." Tad glances in the mirror to fix his photogenic hair, then shimmies closer to me.

"Oops." I grab my tequila a little too fast, sending half the amber liquid sloshing over the edge of the shot glass, so I coach myself to calm down. There's too much at stake. "To getting to know each other better."

"Cheers." He clinks his shot glass against mine, holding it there. His gaze travels from my eyes to my crossed legs and back. "You know what they say… 'All's fair in love and war.'"

"…and justice." I wink, which makes him laugh. My smile is genuine, if not romantic.

After we knock back our shots and chomp on our lime slices, Tad motions the bartender over. While he orders beer chasers for both of us, I snag a wad of nearby napkins to clean up my mess, then place my cell phone down on the bar.

We spend the next few minutes getting our relationship statuses out of the way. He is divorced, no kids, a real estate agent. I've never been married. Currently, between relationships and jobs.

My hands shake, so I hide them under the bar and steer the conversation back to Tad. "You must get recognized a lot."

He purses his lips, but the twinkle in his eyes belies the pride within. "You've seen my billboards?"

"Sure." Who hasn't? His mugshot is plastered on his weekly half-page real estate ads in the local newspaper and every few miles along the highway. Though I don't usually admire show-offs, Tad certainly made himself easy to find online, and for that I'm grateful. "Same photo as your dating profile."

"The publicity is good for business. I sell houses." Tad slides his business card in front of me. "So, what do you do for fun? Date much?"

"This is actually my first online date ever." I slip the card into my shoulder bag for safe keeping. "But lately, I've gotten interested in genealogy. Actually, researching local family trees is what brings me back to South Carolina this time."

"You live out of town?" Tad shifts in his seat and I suspect he couldn't care less about my interests, so I let him change the topic.

"These days, Virginia. But I grew up in the Lowcountry. My parents still live here. I come back every so often to visit and check up on them. They refuse to leave our house."

"Oh, yeah? Which town?" He takes a healthy swig of his beer while I swirl mine. The way he perks up makes me suspect he's mentally calculating his commission if he can convince my parents to sell it. It's not that nice.

"Nowheresville."

"C'mon. I've sold houses on every street within a fifty-mile radius of this bar."

"No way you've heard of it." The way he nudges my shoulder, he probably assumes I'm flirting.

"Try me." He sits up straighter, ready to catch any ball thrown at him. This guy must really like his job.

"Okay." Coy is my middle name. I sip my beer then slap the bottle on the bar with a solid *thunk*. Challenge accepted. "Palmetto Hollow. Back by the creek."

"Shut up." He turns on his stool to face me. "Did you graduate from Oakhill High?"

I nod, then take a swig of my beer to hide my smile. Now I've earned his interest. "Yup. Home of the Fighting Possums. Don't tell me you went there, too…"

"Nah, but I went to every home football game as a kid. My cousin was their star quarterback in the nineties." Tad's eyes lit up like a Christmas tree caught on fire, but he hushed his voice as if he were letting me in on a big secret. "You might have heard of him. Jimmy Flay?"

Score.

"No way! You're cousins with *Touchdown Flay*?" My voice grows loud enough that other patrons glance over at us. I bite my lip to keep from smiling over-hard. This is easier than I expected.

"Keep it down, Corynne. You'll cause a stampede." Tad shushes while sporting a knowing grin. "Don't need everyone in here rushing me for selfies and autographs."

Yeah, right. I glance over my shoulder, but no one seems remotely interested. Whatever.

I fan the flame of Tad's little family tree ego trip.

"I was a few years behind Jimmy in school, but he was all over the Saturday sports pages and TV reports. You know, now that I think about it, you kinda look like him." When I reach to clink our beer bottles, Tad puffs his chest. Not sure if it's because he takes my observation as a compliment, or if he thinks he's going to get lucky tonight. Neither is true. "I heard he got a full ride to the University of Alabama. Did he get drafted to a professional team?"

"No. Jimmy injured his hand midseason as a freshman at Bamma and dropped out of school. It killed his football career."

"That stinks. Jimmy was the brightest star we had around here." The update sobers our date like a cold shower. "So, where's he now? Married with a desk job and two-point-three kids?"

"Hardly." Tad shakes his head but doesn't explain himself.

After an awkward moment, I nudge his shoulder. My eyes couldn't possibly be any rounder with concern. "What do you mean? Is he okay?"

"He ran into problems about ten years ago. Big problems." Tad inches his stool a little closer, his thigh now touching mine, then lowers his voice so only I can hear. "Went off-grid after a local girl went missing."

"Oh, my God. Did he…" I swallow back bile, hardly able to articulate the words. Perspiration beads on my neck. "Did he kill her?"

"No! Nothing like that. But they'd dated a bit, and he didn't have a good alibi, so he decided to skip town until things calmed down. The law always blames the boyfriend." Tad drains his beer. "Jimmy was right. The cops came looking."

"Scary stuff."

"I know, right? By the time the girl's body was found, he was long gone, and his apartment and everything inside had been burned."

"Holy crap. Burned? As in arson?" This fact had been splashed all over the local papers at the time, but I played dumb. "Do you think he started it?"

"Nah, the fire chief could never prove he did either. It was caused by a gas leak in the kitchen." Tad motions the bartender for another drink. "But the timing didn't look good to the cops."

"Who was she?"

"Who?"

"The girl who died." Thank God Tad is looking at his beer and not me as I'd bet money my face is a shade of puke-green.

"Ellen Mc-something. Can't remember her last name. Just some starry-eyed hick a couple years behind him in high school. Jimmy never even brought her around to meet the family, but I heard she had wild red hair." Tad shifts, so his entire side touches mine. It's everything I can do to keep from shoving him away. "Want another drink?"

"No, thanks." Even if I could have one, I'd never be able to keep it down. My stomach churns, just thinking about Ellen and the cruel way she'd suffered.

"Did he ever move back here? You know...after things calmed down?"

"Nah. Jimmy disappeared. No cell phone. They found his wallet and credit cards in the charred remains of the fire. For a long time, the family knew nothing about his whereabouts. But about five years ago, his parents got an unsigned picture postcard from Miami Beach. A couple years after, one from Dallas, and then later one from Atlanta."

"At least you know he's still alive, but with no way to contact him, it must be really tough on your family."

"Don't tell anyone I told you this, but..." Tad gives me a conspiratorial wink, then lowers his voice to a near-whisper. "About a year ago, Jimmy sneaked into his parents' house late one night. He only stayed an hour. My uncle said you'd never recognize him now. He put on fifty pounds, shaved his head, and grew a long beard. He even changed his name to Butch Miller. Said he was hustling odd jobs in Virginia Beach."

I force my eyebrows to relax, and my face to stay neutral. "Did they ever find out who killed the girl?"

"Not that I heard. The investigation hit the papers every once in a blue moon, but after a while, press interest fizzled out with no new leads."

My cell phone pings. The driver of my prearranged ride is waiting outside.

"Mind if we take a selfie? It's not every day a girl gets to have drinks with *Touchdown Flay*'s cousin." As I hold my phone facing us, Tad gives me his real estate billboard smile. Nice enough guy, if a bit self-centered. Not my type. Still, my date with Tad was the best decision I ever made.

Sliding off the stool, I place enough cash on the bar to cover the tequila shots. "My ride's here. It was really nice meeting you, Tad. Thanks for the beer."

"Don't go. The night is still young." His face looks so stricken, my determination falters for a half a second. "Cancel your car service. I can drive you back to your hotel later."

"Thanks, but not this time. I'll let you know next time I'm in town." I flash him an over-bright smile then back away from the bar. "I have an early flight tomorrow morning."

"Can I get your number?"

"I've got your business card." I turn and beeline for the exit door. "Cheers."

I'd been prepared to stay longer, make small talk, but Tad had been easy. I pat my shoulder bag—I have everything I came for.

*

Though it's way past midnight, I've converted my still-made hotel bed into a workshop. My flight home is scheduled for first thing in the morning, so I have a few more hours yet before I have to check out of my hotel. I miss South Carolina, but ten years ago, it broke my heart, so I left. I don't know how my parents can stay here.

Glancing at Tad's business card photo gives me a pang of guilt, which is quashed just as quickly. I have no doubt Tad forgot about me seconds after I walked out the door into the gravel parking lot, then he probably chatted up some other woman at the Hitch & Swig. That's okay. He won't ever see me again. Not outside of a courtroom, anyway.

Tad was merely my pawn.

Jimmy Flay may have eluded the authorities for a decade. Still, criminals hiding from the law aren't the only ones who can change their identity to their advantage. My sundress and the blond wig are now packed at the bottom of my roller bag, my hair returned to my natural ginger. Just like my big sister, Ellen. My red wavy hair would've been a dead giveaway as to who I really am. During the ride back to my hotel, I deleted my faux-profile from the dating app, after saving a screenshot of Tad's. Then I cropped myself out of our selfie.

Corynne isn't my real name, either. It's Tracy.

I was the last person to ever speak to Ellen before she sneaked out of our house to hook up with Jimmy a couple months after he'd moved back home from college. I tried to stop her from going. Her face had been sheet-white. Her hands trembling. I'll never forget her last words to me. *Don't tell Daddy, or I'll be in a shitload of trouble. Wish me luck.*

By the next morning, Ellen and Jimmy were both gone. Missing. News circulated that his apartment had caught on fire. A week later, a runner noticed her red hair in a pile of leaves and called the police. They found Ellen's decomposing body, partially buried, in a local park.

Jimmy killed her. And I know why. After Ellen had disappeared, I foraged through our bedroom for clues. I read her diary. I searched under the bed, in the pockets of her clothes, and through her desk. But it wasn't until I found the positive pregnancy test stick hidden under her pillow that I'd figured it out. The empty box stashed at the bottom of her school backpack was for a two-pack, and the date on the receipt was the same day she disappeared. She must have taken the other test with her that night to show Jimmy.

Their lovers' tryst had turned horribly tragic. The coroner confirmed she'd been strangled and had sustained a gash in her head from a blunt object.

At my big sister's funeral, I vowed to avenge her murder.

I told Daddy my theory. And the police. And the lead detective. But the manhunt turned up empty. Any potential physical evidence that may have been left in Jimmy's apartment had been destroyed. The DNA the police collected at the crime scene didn't have a match in their criminal database.

Without a prior conviction, the state lab didn't even have Jimmy's DNA on file, and by then, he was already on the lam, so the police couldn't collect it. Ellen's case went cold.

Until now.

When I empty the contents of my shoulder bag onto the hotel bed, a sticky shot glass rolls out—the prize I'd traveled back to my hometown to collect. I'd have gone on a dozen blind dates with all of Jimmy's relatives to swipe this evidence for Ellen. Thank God it had only taken one.

Science had changed over these past ten years. Geneticists have been busy researching. Private DNA services have been building their databases thanks to a growing public interest in genealogy. Most customers swab their mouths to discover their origins. But a recent biproduct of the testing service is that these databases have helped investigators zero in on criminals. Where laws, policies, and procedures limit police investigations, now private citizens can help solve cases. Am I treading through ethical and legal gray areas? Sure. But then again, Ellen's murderer still walks free. My motto these days is, all is fair in love, war, and justice.

Finding Jimmy's extended family members wasn't hard. Just a few clicks of a mouse on an ancestor-search website, and I'd reverse-engineered his family tree. As a first cousin by way of Jimmy's dad's side, Tad made my shortlist of candidates to stalk, especially since he was single and on the prowl.

Arranging our date had been even easier. Anyone who would plaster his face on billboard ads craved attention. I prayed that he might get loose-lipped after a few drinks. Though I only needed him to consume one—the tequila shot.

After taping shut and labeling the shipping package, I add FRAGILE in big letters across the box. The DNA processor usually expects kits to arrive with swabs. Still, they assured me that for an extra fee, they could also process other items, such as toothbrushes or drinkware—like a shot glass. I paid cash to buy the prepaid credit card I'm using to pay for the private lab service. I'll swing by on my way to the airport to drop it off at the shipper's self-service station. No need to involve the post office and risk being charged with mail fraud.

With the simple tasks behind me, my next job requires a little more finesse. After logging in to my account on the county's crime-solver webpage for cold cases, I upload a few photo files. Then I draft a message to the lead investigator assigned to Ellen's case.

Dear Detective Jones,

Please find enclosed the following information pertaining to Ellen McCreary's unsolved murder case: a business card of Jimmy Flay's first cousin, a photo of his cousin from the Hitch & Swig Tavern, an audio recording of our conversation with information on Flay's recent whereabouts, and confirmation of his current alias, Butch Miller.

In ten days, the lab results of Jimmy Flay's cousin's DNA will be uploaded on www.DNAmatch.com. I expect the state lab will find a positive familial match to the DNA collected from my sister's crime scene.

Sincerely,
Tracy McCreary

It's taken a decade, but with Jimmy's cousin's DNA on this shot glass plus the clues of Jimmy's current whereabouts with the proper authorities, Ellen's murderer will be brought to justice. Finally.

Tad was just a means to an end.

My only advice to Tad is, be careful next time you swipe right.

MALBEC GOLD
by Frances Aylor

"Try this one." Sofia spun around to hand me a glass of inky purple wine. "I think it's our best yet."

I sniffed the malbec, sipped it, and let it roll around on my tongue. "It's marvelous. I taste fruit. Blackberry, perhaps, and plum? Maybe a touch of smoke?"

She clapped her palms together. "Madeline, I knew you were perfect for this job. You have a good palate."

Sofia managed Nalmaguer Vineyards, her family-owned boutique located in Argentina near the Andes Mountains. The high elevation of the Mendoza region meant warm days and cool nights, perfect growing conditions for the grapes used in her award-winning malbec wines.

Sofia had recently hired my public relations firm to handle the launch of her products into the U.S. market. Our job was to build her brand among oenophiles, those dedicated wine lovers who chatted knowledgeably about vintage and varietals and the relative merits of oak versus stainless steel. They were willing to pay top dollar for special wines to stock in their own climate-controlled wine cellars.

My business partner Lilly had set up this wine tasting at the penthouse apartment of an investment banker friend. The lights of New York City twinkled far below us. She gestured at the elegantly dressed crowd. "They love your wine. Soon Nalmaguer Malbec will be at the top of everyone's list."

I nodded. "Especially when you win a gold at the Iguazu Wine Festival next month." Lilly and I had both signed up to support Sofia and check out her competition. The biggest names in South American wine would be there.

Sofia's green eyes, carefully outlined in black, glittered. "That's my dream. But I warn you, the competition is cutthroat. Be prepared to watch your back."

*

The trip from the Iguazu airport to our hotel took Lilly and me from city streets onto a bumpy narrow road that wound through miles of sprawling green jungle. The leafy trees and arching undergrowth were so thick that a jaguar could have been racing a few feet away from us and we never would have spotted him. The hotel was nestled in a clearing near the river, three stories of weathered wood and glass walls, angled for optimum views of Iguazu Falls. Two additional buildings were under construction near the main one, and we could hear the pounding of hammers and whine of electric saws as our taxi deposited us at the front door.

The evening began with a meet-and-greet. Fortunately for us, most of this group spoke fluent English. Lilly and I moved through the crowd, sipping wine and nibbling hors d'oeuvres as we took pictures for Nalmaguer's social media posts.

We found Sofia talking to a tall man with a gently weathered face and silver hair. "Ladies, I want you to meet Julio Garcia, from Caracteras Vineyard," she said. "He's a neighbor in the Uco Valley, not far from me."

Dressed in a custom-tailored suit, he projected a confident aura of success. "Good to meet you," he said.

"Julio has won a number of awards." Sofia shook back her long dark hair. "He has several wines entered in this competition. A cabernet and some blends, along with a malbec."

He brushed an invisible piece of lint from his sleeve. "I hear your malbec is the one to beat this year."

"So kind of you," she said, with a modest shrug. "We'll see."

We chatted for a few moments. As he walked away, Sofia frowned. "Julio's a big operator, and he wants to buy me out. It's difficult for a small vineyard like mine to compete in global markets. A gold here would help hold him off."

"A gold would be great," I agreed, "but even without that, I'm confident we can grow your U.S. sales. We'll be rolling out your strategy over the next few weeks."

"Good. I'm depending on you," she said. "You know, these competitions are supposed to be blind taste-testing, so the judges don't know who produced the wines. And yet, the big vineyards win year after year." She gave a wry grin. "Which means, either they have much better wine than us little guys, or they somehow are able to influence the judges."

"You think those tastings aren't really blind?" Lilly asked. "That the judges are tipped off?"

"I can't prove that, but there's a lot at stake with these awards." She gestured toward two men standing in a far corner. "See the heavyset man over there in the wire-rimmed glasses? He's Diego Mantigua, another big operator in Mendoza. And the bald man beside him? That's Rubén Barratoda, the owner of this hotel. Rubén sells a lot of Diego's wine in his restaurant. He wouldn't hesitate to put in a good word with the judges to help one of his best suppliers."

"Rubén sells your wine, too, doesn't he?"

"Yes. He carries inventory from most of the competitors here."

Lilly set down her wine. "What are we waiting for? Let's put our own word in Rubén's ear. Tell him how much publicity we can generate for him when you win a gold."

Rubén listened politely to our best pitch, but a flatness in his eyes told me we hadn't won him over. If he did have any influence with the judges, he wouldn't be using it to support Sofia.

The evening ended with tango dancing in the lounge. The men at this conference greatly outnumbered the women, and we easily found partners. Sofia and Lilly were naturals, but I felt awkward, clumsily stepping on the feet of anyone reckless enough to ask me to dance. Signaling to Lilly that I was leaving, I headed to my room, eager to work on my next blog post for Nalmaguer.

*

Breakfast the next morning was on the patio, a large flagstone area set with glass-topped tables and cushioned wicker chairs, all quickly claimed by early risers. The overflow crowd spilled down to the pool area. After filling a plate at the buffet, I spotted Julio and Diego chatting together at a two-top. Sofia's comments last night about the big vintners winning most of the awards had made me suspicious. I headed in their direction, hoping to eavesdrop.

But Lilly had scored a space on the stacked stone wall bordering the carefully landscaped garden, and she waved me over. "Madeline, you shouldn't have left the tango dancing so early last night," she said. "I met the most gorgeous man."

"Why am I not surprised?" I said, sitting beside her. Lilly's unusual combination of auburn hair and blue eyes never failed to attract admirers.

"Seriously, you should see this guy. Sebastian would be perfect as the lead in a steamy telenovela." She flushed like a teenager meeting her favorite superstar. "Dark wavy hair. Sultry, smoldering eyes. Heavy black eyebrows. And a rugged jawline with just a touch of designer stubble."

I speared a piece of mango. "You do remember that we're supposed to be working? Taking pictures? Learning about the competition?"

"No reason we can't mix in a little fun. Sebastian's a waiter here. He gave me a tour last night of the back room, where they set up the wines for the tasting." She sipped her coffee. "Whoa, this stuff is bitter."

I passed her a sugar packet. "Next time ask for café americano. It's more like what we're used to at home."

She emptied the sugar into her mug. "Anyway, the back room is quite an operation. There were hundreds of bottles lining the tables, with rows of stemmed glasses set up in front of each of them. Each glass has a paper tag with a number that corresponds to the bottle being tested."

"Can the judges see the bottles?"

"Nope. The waiters fill the glasses and wheel them out to the dining room. The judges only see the number on each glass, so they can't identify the vineyard." She bit into a flaky medialuna, catching stray pieces of the crispy layers in her plate. "I know Sofia is suspicious that the same vineyards keep winning, but maybe it *is* because their wines are better."

I ate another bite of fruit. "Do you think the judges talk to each other? Try to trade votes so the wine they like best gets a medal?"

"I guess they could," she said. "There are five judges at a table. They sample each wine and then assign a grade. It's possible they could compare notes."

"Do we get to watch? Maybe catch them cheating?"

"Nope. Only the waiters are allowed in the room with the judges. That's why there are so many activities planned for today. Hiking. Boat rides. Horseback riding. To keep the vintners occupied while the judging is going on." She crumpled her napkin. "Sofia signed us up for a boat ride to the falls, something she's always wanted to do. But before we leave, I'll work on her website. See which of my pictures would look best."

A few hours later, Lilly and I met up with Sofia in front of the hotel for our excursion to the falls. After a short bus ride to the river, we joined a group strapping on bright orange life jackets. Sofia waved to a curly-haired man with the compact, muscled body of a soccer player. "Tobias, come join us."

"Sofia." He rushed toward us and hugged her.

"This is my friend Tobias," Sofia said. "We grew up together. Our fathers were best friends." She motioned toward us. "Madeline and Lilly are from New York. They are handling promotion for me, for the U.S. market."

Tobias nodded. "I heard you planned to increase your exports. Your father would have been proud of your success."

"As would yours, Tobias. You've done a good job managing your vineyard."

He flashed an engaging smile. "But you are the one with the malbec everyone is talking about. I am sure you will take a gold in the competition. Maybe even best in show."

"That would be wonderful," she said. "We've worked hard to

improve the quality of our wines over the past years. I know every vine in my fields, when to harvest, how delicately to crush the grapes. But still..." She gestured toward Julio and Diego, who stood near us. "They keep winning the top awards."

The boat captain signaled that our tour was ready to begin. We filed onto the open boat, along with Julio and Diego and others I recognized from last night's cocktail party. There weren't four seats together, so we spread out among the rest of the group.

The enormous waterfalls, taller than Niagara and wider than Victoria, stretched out in every direction. Thundering water poured over towering cliffs. Our boat pitched in the churn as we moved closer and closer to the falls.

The relentless noise unsettled me. It slammed against my skull and burrowed deep into my brain...louder than thousands of screaming Super Bowl fans, louder than the persistent droning of race cars at the Daytona 500, louder than the tonsil-bursting screech of panicked riders on a plunging roller coaster...nonstop and inescapable.

The air grew thick with clinging mist. I clamped my knees around the waterproof bag that held my cell phone and wallet, my only possessions on this boat with any hope of staying dry. Many passengers hooted and laughed as stinging drops pelted into our faces, but the woman across from me seemed as nervous as I was. She squeezed her lips into a thin line and tightened the straps on her life jacket. I could understand why they made us sign liability releases before we boarded.

The captain edged us closer to the pounding water. I held my breath as the heavy spray gushed over my head.

I heard an agonized shriek. Whirling around, I saw Sofia several rows behind me, her hands shielding her nose as the torrent surged over her. "I can't breathe," she yelled. She turned her back to the falls and leaned down, rounding her shoulders to block the deluge. As the boat dipped suddenly in the rough chop, Sofia toppled into the muddy river and sank out of sight.

"Sofia!" I screamed.

She popped to the surface, choking as waves splashed over her face. Someone tossed out a life preserver, but despite her frantic kicking, it floated tantalizingly out of reach. The current pulled her closer and closer to the raging falls. She had only a few minutes before she got sucked under.

I jumped from the boat, my arms digging into the water as I struggled to execute my best freestyle stroke. Grabbing Sofia's wrist, I pulled her toward me and wrapped an arm around her waist. I hooked the other around the life preserver as the boat captain reeled us in.

Strong hands hoisted us out of the water and wrapped us in towels. Sofia hunched over, gasping like a hooked fish. Water dripped from her eyelashes and rolled down her pale face.

Lilly pounded Sofia's back. "Are you all right?"

Sofia shivered and dropped to a seat, clutching her arms to her chest. "That was no accident," she whispered.

Lilly leaned closer. "What? What did you say?"

"That was no accident." Sofia pulled the towel tighter around her shoulders. "Somebody pushed me."

*

Lilly and I wanted the boat captain to hear Sofia's story, and to call in the police to investigate, but Sofia refused. "What could they do?" she said. "There's no proof of a crime. Besides, I want people at this festival to focus on my wine, not on me. If I tell the captain someone tried to kill me, that's all anyone will talk about."

"You can't ignore this," I insisted. "Your life is in danger."

"Madeline, I can't talk about this here. Everyone can hear us." She glanced at the other passengers, who stared curiously at her. "Wait until we get back to the hotel. We can meet up at the bar after I get a hot shower."

She seemed more relaxed when we rendezvoused an hour later. Sofia had three glasses of red wine waiting for us. "I thought we could do our own taste test."

Lilly shook her head as she signaled for the bartender. "Sorry, Sofia, after an afternoon like this, I need more than wine. I'm a martini girl, anyway. If you want to do a taste test, line up Ketel One, Absolut, and Gray Goose. This stuff?" She gestured toward the three glasses. "I can tell if wine is red or white, and that's about it. All that blather about blackberries and smoke is way beyond me."

Sofia laughed. "It takes time to train your palate. At least you're honest about it."

I picked up a glass. "Let's talk about the boat. Who do you think pushed you?"

"I don't know." She sipped one of the wines, then grimaced, holding her hand to her lips. "This wine is terrible. Too much tannin. My tongue is drying out."

"I told you to try a martini." Lilly munched an olive.

"Julio and Diego were both on that boat," I said. "And they've both mentioned how good your malbec is. Do you think they'd try to get rid of you?"

She shrugged. "Maybe. None of my family members is ready to step up and take control of Nalmaguer. Without me, they'd have to sell. And both Julio and Diego want my vineyard."

"You can't let them get away with this," I said. "We have to do something."

"I'll take care of it," Sofia said. "I've known most of the people on that boat for years. Let me handle it my own way."

Lilly gestured to the bartender for another martini. "Okay," she reluctantly agreed. "But the three of us need to stick together. To make sure no one else tries anything."

*

The next morning marked the last day of the competition. After a final round, the judges would announce the medal winners and the hotly anticipated "best in show" award.

Sofia, Lilly, and I decided to walk off our nerves with a hike through the jungle. "Have you heard anything from your friend Sebastian?" I asked Lilly as we started out. "Any clues about which wines are ahead?"

She slapped at a bug on her arm. "No. I haven't seen him. Guess he's busy setting up."

We headed for the nearest trail head. Plastic sheeting flapped as we passed the new construction. "Rubén is adding a lot of rooms," Sofia said. "Business must be good."

At first the trail was broad and well-marked, but it narrowed as we moved deeper into the jungle. Treetops closed over us, blocking the sun and throwing the path into shade. Lilly suddenly stopped short. "Shh. Do you hear that?"

"Hear what?" I said. "That croaking sound?"

"It may be a toucan," Sofia said. "There's lots of them in the jungle."

"It's not a croak. Something else. Kind of a snort." Lilly crouched down, pushing aside the dense undergrowth for a better look.

"Do you see anything?" I asked.

"It's an animal," she whispered. "Furry, sort of reddish brown, with black paws and a long tail. Maybe a raccoon."

I peered through the greenery. "I've never seen a raccoon with a face like that. Do you see the snout on that thing? And how about those claws? They're enormous."

Sofia squatted beside me. "It's a coati. They're common around here." The animal grunted as he dug into the soft earth, tossing up dirt behind him. "He must be looking for dinner."

I kept my voice low. "He's found something." The coati clamped his teeth together and yanked his head to the side.

Lilly grabbed my arm. "Oh, my God, Madeline. Oh, my God."

"What is it?" I shifted my position for a better view.

"It's a hand," Lilly said. "He's dug up a hand."

The three of us rushed toward the animal, screaming. He

hesitated, then scuttled off into the underbrush. A human hand poked from the disturbed earth.

Lilly shrieked, pointing to an elaborate leather braid just below the palm. "Sebastian was wearing a bracelet like that."

Sofia crouched down. "He may still be alive. Maybe we can do CPR." She pressed her fingers against his wrist. "I don't feel a pulse. Help me clean off his face, to see if he's breathing."

We dropped to our knees and brushed the dirt from his face and torso. Lilly groaned. "It *is* Sebastian. Oh, my God, I can't believe this."

Sofia touched his neck. "No pulse." A reddish-brown stain covered the right half of his chest. "He's been shot." She dug through his pockets.

"What are you doing?" Lilly asked.

"Somebody killed Sebastian. Somebody tried to kill me. I want to know why."

Lilly grabbed her arm. "Are you crazy? We shouldn't touch him. We need to call the police."

"Wait. There's something here." Sofia pulled out a crumpled paper and smoothed it against her thigh. "It's a wine label. Two labels, actually, stuck together." She picked at the edges with her fingernail. "My Nalmaguer is on the bottom, covered up with this other label. Looks like someone stuck their label on my malbec, to confuse the judges. They wouldn't realize it was my wine they were sampling."

"But why?" I asked.

"Because somebody thought my malbec would win. They wanted to claim the credit instead of me."

I glanced down at the paper in her hand. "Do you know whose label that is?"

"Yes. And we've got to get back right now, to stop him."

"Wait, we have to call the police," Lilly said. "We can't leave Sebastian here all alone."

Sofia pulled out her phone. "There's no service out here," she said. "I'll call when we get to the hotel."

*

We raced through the jungle to the hotel, running through the lobby, the patio, and the pool area.

"I don't see him," Sofia said. "Let's go down to the wine cellar."

Sofia called the police to report Sebastian's murder. Then we slipped around back to the kitchen entrance. "This way," Sofia said, pointing toward a darkened stairway.

The three of us crept down the steps. Cool moist air hit our faces as Sofia eased open a heavy door. The dimly lit room contained endless rows of towering shelves, all filled with wine bottles. We worked our way through the maze toward murmuring voices.

Two men stood in the shadows. I saw Rubén's bald head. "I've done what you wanted," he said. "Now give me the money."

"Not until they've announced the winners," the second man said.

"I can't see the other guy," I whispered to Sofia. "Do you know who it is?"

She nodded, biting hard on her lower lip.

"I never promised you'd win," Rubén said. "I agreed to put your label on her wine."

"That won't do me much good if it doesn't get the gold."

Rubén poked the other man in the shoulder. "I put in a good word with the judges, just like you wanted. Don't try to change our agreement now. The bank is pressuring me to get current on my construction loans for those new buildings. I need the cash."

Sofia walked out from our hiding place behind the shelves. "I can't believe you would do this to me."

They both whirled toward her voice. I recognized the curly hair of Tobias. "Sofia, let me explain," he said.

"We grew up together, Tobias. Our fathers were best friends. Why would you do this?"

His shoulders slumped. "I needed a winner, Sofia. You know how difficult it is for small vineyards like ours to make a profit. My wines haven't won a medal in three years. I have to turn things around before I lose everything."

"And you, Rubén," she said. "When word gets out about this, no one will do business with you."

"That's why no one can know." Rubén pulled out a gun.

Sofia backed away, holding up her hands. "I know you don't want to shoot me."

He aimed the gun at her chest. With only a few feet between them, there was no way he could miss. I had to act fast. Grabbing a wine bottle, I jumped from behind the shelving and slammed the bottle hard against Rubén's head. He staggered to the floor.

Lilly grabbed another bottle and stomped toward Tobias. "Face down on the floor," she said, "or we'll knock you out, too.

Sofia knelt beside Rubén. "He's alive, but he'll have one beast of a headache when he wakes up." She turned to Tobias. "You pushed me out of the boat, didn't you? You tried to kill me."

"It was a warning," he said. "I never meant for you to drown."

"What kind of a warning was that? I'd be dead if Madeline hadn't jumped in to rescue me."

Lilly slammed her foot into Tobias's back. "What about Sebastian? We found his body. Did you kill him?"

"Not me. Rubén. Sebastian caught him switching wine labels." Tobias grunted as Lilly pushed down harder. "We thought nobody would spot that grave. How did you find him?"

"A hungry coati." Sofia stood up. "Madeline, can you and Lilly watch these guys until the police get here?"

"Of course," I said. "But where are you going?"

"I need to get to the judges before they announce the winners. Explain what happened."

"You think you can fix this?"

"Probably not. But the reputation of this competition is

important to Julio and Diego. If there's been cheating, they may want to use their influence to help." She headed for the door. "Who knows? I might even win a gold."

EVERUS
by K.L. Murphy

The sound of the waves lapping against the side of the boat makes my skin crawl. I take small breaths to steady my nerves, but it's not much help. The engines roar to life, and I grip the railing with both hands. The boat picks up speed. I stare back at the land, pressing my lips together, my stomach already twisting. The marina grows smaller and smaller until it's only a speck on the horizon. If I'd wanted to change my mind, it's too late now.

"What's wrong with you?" Alan asks.

"Nothing." I scoot back from the edge, my hands now firmly closed around my life jacket. "I'm not a water person. That's all."

"But you're not in the water."

I point at the glass bottom where fish dart to and fro under a thick acrylic floor. "Water."

He laughs out loud. "I can't believe you, Cara."

He walks away, and my face flames. It's only the second day of our vacation and already he's had enough of me. Finding a seat on a bench, I tuck my bag under my feet. A group of kids in pink and blue tie-dyed t-shirts shuffle after a woman wearing a whistle. Giggling, they form a circle over the glass bottom. I slump lower. Apparently, even a group of six-year-olds are more fearless than me.

"I couldn't help overhearing."

I jump, startled to find I'm not alone. An old man has settled next to me. "Excuse me?"

He grips the head of a wooden cane with gnarled hands and nods toward the dark water. "Must be hard for you. Being on a boat. Not being a water person."

My shoulders tighten. *Not being a water person.* That's an understatement. No one gets it, not even my own mother. At seventy, she still swims every day.

"My Margie was no good with water either," he says. I shift toward him now. "There was a time when I tried to get her past it—like your young man—but I gave up in the end. Now, I get out on the water as much as I can." His cloudy eyes slide to mine. "I'd stay on dry land though, if I could get Margie back."

"I'm sorry," I say, although I have no idea what I'm sorry for.

"She's been gone two years now. Cancer got her. Could've been worse, I guess. Was quick at least. None of that hogwash where they put poison in you to make you better. They called it stage four, but it was more like a five or six. Didn't last a month after we found out."

I don't know what to say to that either, so I apologize again.

"Yep. That's what everyone says." He taps his cane as he talks. "But I'm the sorriest. Shouldn't have cared about the water thing. We'd fight, and she'd cry. For a lotta years, she wouldn't tell me why. Her cousin finally told me. Made sense then."

I stare at him openly now. A man who understands—even if it's taken years and a dead wife. I'm not sure Alan will ever get there. "What was it, if you don't mind my asking?"

"It doesn't matter now," he says, his mouth pursed. I disagree—it matters very much to me—but I let it go. "I started making these trips, spending more time on the water after she died. The funny thing is, I don't love it the way I used to."

"Why do you do it then? If you don't love it, I mean."

He lifts a bony shoulder. "Because she'd want me to. When she got the cancer, she made me promise I would do all the things I couldn't before. After she died, I signed up for a cruise. Then I went up to Niagara Falls just to see it. I've gone fishing. Sat on a dozen beaches." His gaze sweeps past the families crowded around the boat. "This tour was on my list back when she was alive. I wanted her to see the fish. I'm too old to snorkel now, but they promise that doesn't matter."

"That's what my fiancé said, too."

"Guess you're not snorkeling then either?"

I give him a small smile. "Not today." Alan had done his best to convince me to come anyway. "You don't even have to get in the water," he'd said. "You can stay safe and dry in the boat and still see the fish through the glass. They can't touch you." He'd made it sound so reasonable, so easy, and he'd smiled in that way that made me shiver. Against my better judgment, I'd agreed. What did it get me? I'm sitting with a complete stranger, and Alan is nowhere to be found.

The crowd parts in front of us. A young woman staggers forward, her body out of sync with her legs. In one hand, she clutches a red plastic cup. In the other, a flowered backpack. Her white-blond hair hangs loose over her face and shoulders, and the short red dress she's wearing rides high up her thighs. She teeters on matching red wedges, wobbles, and nearly falls on the old man before catching herself. She slurs something that sounds like an apology, but the words are hard to understand.

"Perhaps you should be more careful, young lady," my new friend says. The girl's head comes up. Her eyes, unfocused and red-rimmed, land on the old man. "You could have hurt one of us." He gestures in my direction. "Or yourself."

Her gaze wanders from him to me. She seems to still. Her mouth forms a circle and she sways on her tall shoes.

"Are you with anyone?" I ask. "I could try to find them for you."

The woman blinks, then erupts into laughter. She gets the hiccups which only makes her laugh harder. Tears run down her cheeks. The teacher herds the children back toward the railing. From the corner of my eye, I catch sight of one of the boat's staff pushing his way through the crowd.

Her laughter dies. She raises her hand and some of whatever was in her cup spills onto my toes. "I like your necklace," she says, the words running together.

My fingers find the gold chain around my neck.

She raises her cup again and stumbles away. In a moment, she's swallowed up by the other passengers. The man from the boat turns away.

"Well, someone hit the bar before noon," the man next to me says.

I force a small laugh, although I'm not amused. My fingers caress the necklace she'd liked. It had been an engagement present from Alan. I'd tried to tell him I didn't need another gift. "Look at this ring," I'd said, holding out my hand. "It's beautiful enough. You didn't need to get me a necklace, too." The ring is beautiful in its way, but the large square diamond surrounded by more diamonds isn't really my taste. My first husband had given me an opal. We didn't have much money in those days, but even after we did, I'd refused to trade up. I wear it on my right hand now. I do love the necklace though. It's custom. A simple gold chain with a single word. *EverUs*. Well, not really one word, but sort of. It's corny, of course. Daniel, my first husband, would never have purchased such a thing. But Alan is young and an artist. He's romantic that way.

The death of my first husband came as a shock to family and friends. The police claimed he was driving drunk. That was shock enough. Before that night, he was known to have a two-drink limit, but his blood-alcohol level said otherwise. There were skid marks on the road as though he'd tried to stop and failed. The car hit the guard rail, buckled, and flipped. Daniel was thrown fifty feet. Apparently, he wasn't wearing his seatbelt. Another shock.

The police came around a few times. I tried to be understanding. They had a job to do. Daniel was a wealthy man by then, and we didn't have any children. Naturally, I inherited most of the estate. What I didn't inherit was given to charity. He was good that way. After a while, the police stopped coming. My mother, the only family I have left, went back to Arizona. Friends came by less and less. Months passed. I was alone. Rudderless. Alan pulled me out of all that.

"We're almost there," the old man says.

I look out to see a semicircle of large rocks rising from the sea.

My insides feel squishy, and I gulp the salty air. The tour guide steps to the front of the boat.

"We're going to anchor soon. As a reminder to those of you snorkeling, we'll sound the horn three times when we need you to head back to the boat. You may snorkel on this side of the rocks only. Don't worry, there's plenty of room for everyone. For those of you staying on the boat, be sure to watch for the fish swimming under the glass. They put on quite a show. You'll also see some of our famous coral."

When she puts down her bullhorn, would-be snorkelers line up at the ladder. Nearby, the children huddle over the glass bottom while their teacher hands out snacks and waters. I scan the line of people holding their masks and flippers. No Alan. I stand up, craning my neck. There's a second line at the rear of the boat and several bodies already bobbing in the water. Although disappointed, I'm not surprised. Alan had been talking about this since we booked the trip. "This reef is one of the best anywhere. It's known all over the state." No doubt, he'd been first in line to get in the water.

"I don't suppose you want to join the children at the glass," the man asks.

"No thanks," I say, shaking my head. "You go ahead though."

"To tell you the truth, I'm not sure my heart's really in it." We sit in silence for a moment. "You're engaged." He tips his head toward my ring.

"Yes. This," I say, waving my hand at the boat, "is sort of a pre-honeymoon."

"Congratulations." He taps his cane again. "I always wonder how young people meet these days. Seems like it was so much simpler in my day. Now, it's all gadgets and those blind date sites or whatever they are. E-love or something."

The old man makes me laugh. It's the best I've felt since we boarded. "I can't disagree with you. It wasn't like that though. Alan's an artist. I met him at an opening at a gallery I go to quite a lot."

"That sounds nice. How was his show?"

"Oh, it wasn't his show. Alan's still working on his collection."

"I see."

I flinch. He sounds like my mother. I consider going over to the glass after all, but I change my mind. Instead, I do what I always do. "It takes a long time to do one painting. Sometimes a year. Alan says there's only one left to finish before he's ready to show."

"Painting, huh? Never been into art myself. Probably because I can't draw my way out of a paper bag." He chuckles as he says this, and I relax again. "Margie though, she did love a good museum." A heavy sigh escapes and he lowers his head. "It's hard sometimes. Her being gone. Kinda thought I would go first to tell you the truth."

"I'm a widow, too. My husband died in a car crash a year ago."

The lines that split his wiry brows deepen. "A year," he says.

I lift my chin. It's not the first time I've gotten this reaction. Even the police showed up again after the announcement in the paper. I tell myself Daniel would want me to be happy, but I'm aware how it looks. "I was a mess after Daniel died," I say, although I don't know why I feel the need to explain. Perhaps it's because the old man reminds me of my father. "We didn't have any children, and I was in that house all alone, and…" My words drift away, like a child's waiting to be forgiven for disobeying. I touch the opal ring on my right hand and brush the prongs with the tip of my finger.

Neither of us speak for a minute. When he does, his voice is different. It's sadder, broken in a way that I recognize. It's the voice of someone who wishes they'd done better, been better. "Margie was only a girl when it happened. About seven, I think. I knew about her sister Mary. 'Course I knew, but I shoulda asked." His knotted hands bring the cane up to his chest. His head drops so that I have to lean closer to hear. "The sisters had gone for a bike ride together out near the pond at the edge of town. It was late in the season, but Margie had begged her sister to take her. Promised to do her chores the next day. Kid stuff, you know."

I nod.

"Anyway, they swam around a little and then got out. It was a nice day. The sun wasn't setting yet, so they decided to lie down on the grass and dry off before heading home." He lifts his head again, and I see the shimmer in his eye. "Margie fell asleep. When she woke up, her sister was gone."

My heart skips a beat. "What do you mean gone?"

"Mary's bike was right where she'd left it, but she was nowhere to be found. It was getting dark by then, so Margie rode home as fast as she could. Her parents did their best not to panic. They went back to the pond with flashlights, thinking maybe Mary had wandered into the woods and gotten lost or hit her head. Something. Anything other than what they feared. By the next morning, dozens of folks had joined in the search. The police brought in the dogs. For two weeks, they looked for Mary, widening the circle each day. Nothing. It was like she disappeared into thin air. Two other girls went missing that summer." He rolled his head from side to side. "Margie blamed herself."

"She was only a child."

"That's true, but just the same, Margie never got over it. Mary was thirteen, a pretty girl excited about starting eighth grade and going to the fall dance. She didn't want to hang out with her little sister. Margie had begged her, promising to do those chores. After that day, Margie never went near water again. Her parents either. They would drive the long way around to avoid the pond. They stopped going to the lake up in Minnesota."

"That's horrible."

"Yep. And I had no idea. Margie couldn't even talk about Mary without crying. I wasn't much good in those times. Usually gave her space to work it out. When her cousin told me, it all made sense."

"You couldn't have known."

He doesn't say anything to that. I look out across the boat to the rocks and the sea. Bodies float face down over the ocean with only those bright colored plastic tubes sticking up out of the water. I shiver.

"What about you?" the old man asks. "Why do you have a thing about water?"

I don't want to tell him. He seems like a kind man and his story is heartbreaking. My own fear is nothing like that. "It's kind of embarrassing."

He stretches his legs and shrugs. "Up to you."

I cringe at his tone. I've never been good with father types. They always make me feel bad—like I've disappointed them in some way. Daniel was older when we married. He asked me then if the age difference bothered me. I didn't think it did at the time.

I look up at the marshmallow-like clouds floating overhead and take a deep breath. "I was ten. Playing in the ocean. My parents were on the beach waving at me. I pretended not to see them and floated out a little further. I could still hear them shouting at me. They weren't calling me to come in. They were pointing and so I turned around. Behind me was the biggest set of waves I'd ever seen." My hands are shaking as I speak.

"That must have been terrifying."

"My mother started to wade in. I wasn't a good swimmer like she was, but even I knew she wouldn't get to me in time. My mother cupped her hands around her mouth." Without thinking, I raise my hands in the same way. "Go under," I say, lost in the memory. "She kept yelling it over and over. I dove under as fast as I could. The water pounded and swirled like a tornado over my head. The sound. It was so loud. God, it was loud. I held my breath as long as I could, but it just kept coming. When it finally settled, I shot up as fast as I could, gasping for breath. But I wasn't swept away. My mother was right. I was fine."

"It was good advice."

"Yes. And as scary as it was, I felt invincible in that moment. Like no wave could ever get me. I was practically dancing my way back to shore. Both my parents were there, waiting for me. That's when I felt it." I pause and my fingers fold into tight fists. "A fish.

Not huge, but big enough. It was inside my bathing suit, flopping, trying to get out. I screamed. I tried to get my suit off, but my hands wouldn't work. The fish was sliding down my stomach and I could feel the little fins flapping. Next thing I knew, I was naked on the beach and this fish—this slimy, hideous fish—was on the sand trying to get back to the water." I shudder and my heart pounds in my ears.

"A fish," I hear him say.

"My parents just stood there, doing nothing. Then they started laughing. Laughing. Can you believe that?"

"Yes, uh no," he says, stuttering. I glance over at him, but he's facing away from me now. He's staring at the girl, the drunk one in the red dress. The fabric clings to her body, and water drips from her hair. She's standing with her back to us, her legs spread apart— half leaning over the rail. Her shoulders are shaking, and I can't be sure if she's crying or throwing up. I think about asking if we should go help her, but I don't get the chance. "So, it wasn't the big waves that made you afraid of the water?"

"No."

"It was the fish in your suit."

"Yes."

He runs his hand over his chin. "What about pools? They don't have fish."

"Doesn't matter. When I was in high school, this boy thought it would be cute to push me in. I had a full-blown panic attack."

"I'm sorry."

"Nothing to be sorry about," I say. The drunk woman is gone. Only the children remain. I point to the mostly empty deck. "Guess it's just us landlubbers left now."

A scream from the circle of children makes us both look up. There's a second scream and a third. They jump to their feet and point. The smallest kids back away from the glass.

The teacher is standing off to the side with one of the boat staff.

"It's probably a shark," I hear her say.

The old man gets up and leans on his cane. "I'm going to see what all the fuss is about."

I watch as he slides past the children. His back arches and stiffens. When he turns around, his ruddy face has paled. "Kids," he says, "why don't you move away and stand with your teacher." He waves the boat staffer over. I can't hear what they're saying, but the younger man stares wide-eyed at the bottom of the boat, shaking his head. He unclips his walkie talkie, holds it to his mouth. Within a minute, three more staff are standing over the glass bottom. The old man says something else, and they turn toward me in unison. Fear snakes up my belly. One of the staff starts in my direction, but the old man stops him.

He sits down next to me, but I don't meet his gaze. I don't dare.

"It's your friend. Your fiancé," he says. "Something happened, and he got tangled in some line and dragged under the boat."

I don't breathe.

"The authorities have been alerted. They're on their way."

"Is he…" A hard lump lodges in my throat, and I can't speak, can't ask what I already know.

"I'm sorry," he says. "He's gone." He's still talking, but I only hear snatches of what he says. "Extra boats. Get the body. Be here for a while." I stagger to my feet and stumble forward. Even through the thick plexiglass, the ocean is the color of an emerald, brilliant and clear. Alan's face stares back at me from under the boat, his brows raised and his mouth parted as though in surprise. Blue and yellow fish peck at his shirt and his hair and his hands. I scream then. I fall to the floor of the boat and scream and scream and scream.

The hours after are a blur. The police come in speedboats. They pull Alan's body out and load it into another boat with flashing lights. More police come to escort us all to shore. They take over the offices at the marina. One by one, they interview every person who'd been on the boat—even the children. The old man stays with me. We wait together, a uniformed policeman hovering nearby. I sit on the hard bench, my body weary, and stare at the giant ring on my left hand. Alan had gone into debt for that ring. "I'm a struggling artist," he'd said when I'd asked him about it. "You don't mind, do you?" I did and I didn't. Although we didn't talk much about the money I'd inherited, I'd grown weary of his assumptions. I'd told the old man the truth. I'd met Alan at a gallery. But it wasn't after my husband's death. It was before.

The door to the cabin opens and an officer steps out. He nods at the old man, and I sit, still waiting. I will be last, of course. I see his gaze skim past me. Mascara stains mark my cheeks. My hair is mussed, and my hands shake as I clutch my bag. The very image of the grieving fiancé.

The old man rises and pats me on the shoulder, but he's not looking at me. The woman in the red dress steps out from behind the officer. She's no longer carrying her red cup, but she's still unsteady on her feet. "Sleep it off," the detective says, his tone half-command, half-leer.

"Sure thing," she says.

The old man walks by her, taking his time. He disappears into the room and the door closes again. The woman stands there, unmoving.

The policeman in the corner clears his throat. "Do you need something, miss?"

"What are you offering?" He frowns and crosses his arms over his chest. She half-laughs and pulls out a cigarette. "Got a light?" she says to me.

"Is it dark?" I ask.

"Not anymore." Her chin comes up and her hair falls away from her shoulders. She touches a hand to her neck, to the custom gold necklace that caresses her skin. She smiles. *EverUs.*

THE NIGHTCAP
by Diane Fanning

At 4 a.m., Laura's cell phone alarm snapped her awake. Before she opened her eyes, she feared she would not remember everything she needed to do. She worried that she'd only imagined the night before. She lifted her lids and observed one item that convinced her it was not a dream: a margarita glass with salt still on the rim and a puddle of condensation on the surface of the table. The watery remains of the cocktail with a limp slice of lime was no longer inviting.

She became aware of the weight on the other side of the bed and turned slowly in that direction. She had to admit to herself, she understood why her ex-husband Jimbo was attracted to that woman. Even dead, with dried vomit around her mouth, Brittany was a beautiful young thing. Her long, natural blond hair splayed across the pillow. Just beyond her, an empty margarita glass sat on her nightstand. Laura double-checked for Brittany's pulse. Nothing.

Last night, Laura thought her set-up wasn't going to work. She didn't get near to Brittany until the woman had consumed a couple of drinks. She introduced herself to the slightly tipsy Brittany as Polly Chambers, the older student from her Medieval Literature class. The drink-befuddled woman said, "Oh right! Yes, yes, yes, I remember you. I'm so glad you could make it." Brittany had fallen in line like a puppet, introducing her to others the same way.

Laura thought Brittany's bachelorette party was absolutely debauched and totally boring. Nonetheless, she smiled all the way through, even stuffing a twenty into the waistband of the tragically predictable dancing cop. After the party was over, it was pathetically easy to lure Brittany into the bar for one more drink. She objected at first, thinking she had to drive, until Laura reminded the young woman that she had a room upstairs in the hotel.

Laura led her to a corner booth, as far from the bar as possible, before fetching the drinks and delivering them to the table. Then, Laura pulled the stupid trick and Brittany fell for it. "Oh, doesn't that guy over there look a lot like Jimbo." She looked and Laura poured her grandmother's liquid heart medicine into Brittany's glass. While doing so, Laura congratulated herself for scooping up that bottle when Nana passed away last year.

Laura's hatred for Brittany knew no bounds. Seven happy years of marriage wiped out by Brittany's flirty ways. Only 22 years old and with the kind of body that could have snared any man, she had to pick on Jimbo. Now Brittany had paid for her sins. And Jimbo? Laura was certain he'd come crawling back to her as soon as he learned of Brittany's death.

Laura knew everything had unfolded as she planned the night before and now she had to get busy with the rest of the scenario. She jumped out of bed, pulled on black pants, a blue silk blouse, suede flats and a pair of latex gloves. Grabbing the two glasses, she carried them into the bathroom. She poured the contents into the sink, thoroughly rinsed the glasses and wiped them off, and took great care not to miss a centimeter of the surfaces. She slid them both into the dry-cleaning bag she'd found in the closet. She had meant to bring a bag from home but forgot. That was her only screw-up so far and she managed to improvise through that.

Laura slipped out of the room, double-checking that the key was in her pocket before shutting the door. Downstairs, the lobby was quiet. She wouldn't have to make a circuitous crossing of the lobby since no one was behind the front desk. She speed-walked to the bar, removed the glasses from the bag and set them on the surface of the counter.

She returned to the room, relieved in her certainty that no one had seen her anywhere along the way. She wiped the surfaces of everything in the suite: in the sitting area, the bedroom and the bathroom—even things she did not think she had touched. She could not afford sloppy assumptions.

She sat down and watched the morning news for an hour before leaving the room again. Before exiting, she double-checked Brittany's pulse and hung the do-not-disturb sign on the outside doorknob. Walking down the hall, she pulled off the latex gloves and stuffed them into the dry-cleaning bag. She ran through her mental checklist of things she needed to do. So far, so good. Laura only had one regret. Now that she was dead, Brittany could not know she'd been outsmarted, and that Laura got her suitable revenge. If she had survived, Brittany would hesitate before stealing another woman's husband ever again.

In the elevator, the jittery anticipation of success danced in Laura's gut. She struggled to eliminate all outward appearances of excitement. All she had left on her to-do list was simple. Walk out of the building to the parking lot across the street. Continue two blocks until she reached the dumpster behind the convenience store. Toss in the bag she used to transport the glasses. Circle the block and stop at the Starbucks on the corner. Go into the restroom and ditch the wig. Buy a grande latte. Walk another two blocks to the hotel where she had a room.

So easy and not one suspicious moment in the bunch—except the visit to the dumpster, but she was confident that she could make it appear normal. When she entered the lobby of her hotel, anyone who saw her would assume she'd gone out for coffee and was now returning. In her room, there were just a few things she would need to do: rumple the bed to make it look as if she spent the night there, take a shower, get dressed, remove the do-not-disturb sign, and leave for home.

As the elevator descended, taking her away from the dead girl she left, her spirits rose higher. She did it. She actually did it and no one would ever know. Anyone who saw her with Brittany last night would describe another blond in an evening dress. She was exultant at her success. The hard part was done. Nothing could defeat her now. She strode out of the elevator feeling like a champion. All her fantasies of revenge had come to marvelous fruition.

Four steps from the revolving door that would take her out of the building and away from danger, she froze in place when she heard the sound of her name. She closed her eyes, hoping that someone had called out to another Laura—it was, after all, a common name. She took one more step to the exit and heard it again.

"Laura! Laura! Is that you Laura?"

A hand touched her forearm, and she was forced to turn in the direction of the voice. She thought about denying her identity until she saw the smiling face of her ex looking right into her eyes.

"Laura, what have you done to your hair? I hardly recognized you," Jimbo asked. "What, in heaven's name, are you doing here?"

BUCKET LIST DREAMS
by Debra H. Goldstein

"I want you to get rid of my husband."

Burke Williams rolled the cigar in his left hand, feeling its fine firm texture. No soft spots or lumps. He figured the brunette sitting on the other side of his polished oak desk, much like his late wife, had a lot of the same characteristics as a good cigar. "That's not exactly my line of business. Murder isn't part of the basic job description for a private eye."

She placed a well-manicured hand on his desk. Her polish was subdued. Somewhere between mauve and pink, but not really either. It matched her tailored business suit and showed off the diamond gracing her ring finger. He liked that she didn't soften the masculine line of the suit with a bow or scarf. The ring, which he eyed as being somewhere between four and five carats, accomplished that.

Burke shifted the cigar to his other hand and picked up the clipper lying in the oversized glass ashtray on his desk. On the day Maggie made him her business partner and husband, she threw away his cheap stogies and gave him the cigar clipper and ashtray. He missed her.

"Please, don't," the woman said as Burke used the double blade clipper to snip the end of his cigar. "Cigarette smoke gives me headaches and cigars just do me in."

"Like you want me to do to your husband, Ms....?"

"Mrs. Mrs. Harold Taylor." She sat back in his guest chair. Burke guessed she was waiting to see his reaction to the "Boxed Wine King's" given name, but he kept his face masklike. She had to know there probably wasn't anyone who'd ever watched TV in the state who hadn't seen Taylor's commercials or didn't know how he'd gone from growing up as a foster care kid to becoming the Boxed Wine King.

He had several commercials, all featuring beautiful people with half-filled wine glasses. Burke's favorite was the one where the Boxed Wine King, in a black mariner's cap and white cable-knit sweater, flanked by four or five beauties, sat staring at a picture-perfect seascape. Together, the group extolled the virtues of the sand, sea, and the ease of bringing a box of Taylor wine wherever they were. Thanks to Taylor's humor, the public's hope of possibly meeting someone like one of his models, and the fact that for $10.99 a box of his wine wasn't bad, he was one of the wealthiest men in the state.

Burke lay the clipper and cigar back into the ash tray. He might not have her money or much prospect of any, but he could play the silence game as well as Mrs. Taylor.

Finally, shifting to a more erect position, she spoke. "Perhaps you've heard of my husband?"

"In passing. I haven't seen any new ads for a year or so."

"That's because he's got dementia. His cognitive issues make taping more commercials impossible."

"I'm sorry to hear that. Dementia's a lousy thing." Having once read up on all fifty-six varieties of dementia for a case he had, he knew what Taylor, and for that matter, his wife, were in for. Lousy for Taylor. Rotten for Mrs. Taylor. But not enough for a private dick to cross the line from investigation to murder.

He wasn't sure which was a worse ending—losing your mind or being eaten alive like Maggie was by cancer. It didn't really matter. Unlike the things he should have manned up and done for Maggie, he didn't owe the lady sitting in front of him anything.

This case smelled, and after his last clash with the local authorities, he couldn't afford to get involved in anything that reeked more than a lit cigar. He ran a finger across his still waiting friend, while his focus remained on Mrs. Taylor's face. He wanted to see if her gaze met his.

It didn't. She appeared to be watching his moving finger.

"I don't see how I can help you. Killing people isn't my business."

She reached into the tote bag she'd dropped on the floor and pulled out a folded newspaper. From the picture poking out above her hand, he knew which article had caught her attention even before she shared it with him.

It was the *Journal* interview attorney Robert Dane gave as a veiled kick-off for his campaign for state attorney general. Normally, Burke ignored run-of-the mill political propaganda, but this one had been personal.

The article painted Maggie as a glittering diamond of the legal community who, at a vulnerable time in her life, was taken advantage of by a loved one. If elected, Dane vowed prosecution of Burke for Maggie's death, as well as going after anyone else who harmed the elderly or the ill. While mainly campaign rhetoric, the article sprinkled indirect suggestions about Burke being a gigolo amidst direct quotes about euthanasia and opioid overdoses. It ended by guaranteeing that a vote for Dane would ensure a voice against opioid abuse and mercy killing.

The middle portion of the interview was burnt into Burke's mind as clearly as the picture Dane staged in front of the flophouse Burke had lived in after walking out on Maggie. It was where she was found dead. Pointing behind him, Dane expressing disgust for how a husband and individual who worked within the law could have sunk below the boundaries of both.

Dane conveniently forgot to mention Maggie had come to the flophouse, dragged Burke off the bed, and then made him shower, shave, and promise to give up booze. Or that, after promising to turn over a new leaf, Burke left Maggie resting on his unmade bed while he went to get them some sandwiches. Despicable liar that he was, Burke stopped to buy a box of Taylor wine. The guy at the liquor store and the time on the receipt were what unraveled the case against him.

Burke waved his hand in the direction of the paper. 'I'm sorry if you got the wrong impression. That article misrepresented the circumstances so badly they printed a retraction."

"I must have missed it."

He wasn't surprised. It ran on page twenty-four.

She tapped the paper. "Even so, what is here, tells me you understand my situation."

"Maybe, but like I said before, I'm not about to jeopardize my license by killing someone."

"You won't be jeopardizing anything, and you'll be well-paid." She reached into her tote again, retrieving a white security envelope.

Burke wondered why she'd bothered with a security envelope when she left it unsealed.

As she dropped it on his desk, he saw the few bills poking out were hundreds.

"I don't want you to actually kill him. I want you to help me kill him with kindness."

"Excuse me?"

"You're a private investigator for hire, aren't you?" She didn't wait for him to answer. "I want you to protect my husband while helping him live out his bucket list."

"Now, I'm the one who doesn't understand."

"It's quite simple. I love Harold or at least I loved the Harold I married. Unfortunately, a lot of his thoughts concentrate on pleasurable things he enjoyed in the past and things he wished he'd done. I want you to help me check things off his bucket list before he can't…"

She rested her hand under her chin. The glint of the solitaire gracing most of her ring finger again caught his eye. He wondered how he missed seeing it was a marquise cut when he sized her up earlier. Maybe because he'd been comparing the size of her diamond with the small round one he'd given Maggie.

"Can you tell me there was never a day when your wife was ill that you didn't wonder how you could extricate the two of you from the situation you were in?"

He desperately wanted his cigar. She was getting too close to feelings he fought against remembering. Burke forced himself to meet her gaze.

"Never."

"Then you're a better person than me." She turned her head away from him and brushed under her eye with the forefinger of the hand with the rock on it.

Burke couldn't decide if she wiped a tear away or was simply acting for his benefit. Either way, the moment passed, and she looked at him again. "There are days I need a distraction."

"How about shopping or a movie?"

"Don't be flippant. That's not what I mean."

She gave him a look that made him think she might be reconsidering her presence in his office but picked up where she'd left off. "I can sit outside with Harold, hold his hand, or stroll our garden with him. I can even wipe drool from his chin. Every day when I do these things, with my good-wife smile pasted on my face, each of us dies a bit more. That's why I want to do something special for us now."

Hence, the bucket list, Burke thought. Did he sense some guilt there, too?

"Wouldn't a round of tennis do for you? Surely, the wife of the Boxed Wine King can afford hired help. You could duck out for a few hours each day to work out, play tennis, go to the beauty salon, or get to know the tennis pro?"

"That's not my style. I took a vow of in sickness or in health when I married Harold. I intend to stand by it, but I need to do something with my mind while he loses his."

Burke understood. He'd tried alcohol before moving out. Maybe her idea was a better way—that is, unless she tried to go from make believe to reality.

"How did you come up with this killing kindly idea?"

She smiled. It was engaging. Somehow, she managed to press her lips together, but show a hint of her teeth. Unlike Maggie's, which had had a slight gap between the two front ones, Mrs.

Taylor's were perfectly uniform. He figured they were capped.

"I asked him what things were still on his bucket list. He said he wished that before a friend died, they'd visited the places they loved as children. When he told me about how they watched seagulls soar at the beach and grabbed for the Watch Hill Flying Horse Carousel's brass ring, I decided to arrange for Harold to visit those places again."

She stood, her hand on the newspaper. "We both know how easily people jump to the wrong conclusions. I had an MBA when I went to work for Harold's company. Most folks think I married him for the benefits that came with being his trophy wife. None of them credit Harold with having been impressed with my brains and abilities. They discount we married for love."

Burke eyed his cigar again. "Love isn't always everything it's cracked up to be."

"Maybe not, but it was for us. Whether he was rich or not, I'd have married him."

"If you love him so much, why don't you simply take him to these places?"

"Now that I'm running the company, I don't have that kind of time. Besides, call me paranoid, but I want to make sure no one harms Harold during his trip down memory lane."

"So, hire an attendant who drives. It's a lot cheaper and makes more sense than hiring a private detective."

"He has an aide. The problem is his attendant, without a gun and the right reflexes, can't keep him safe. I think someone is trying to harm him."

Burke frowned. He'd heard this broken record before. "Why?"

"About a month ago, Harold and his helper planned to spend the day where Harold filmed his beach commercial. Have you seen that ad?"

"Yes." Mrs. Taylor didn't need to know that he was well acquainted with the white sand and pristine water in the ad. He'd spent many pleasant afternoons on that beach with Maggie.

"Apparently, Harold's aide parked near the beach. When they went to cross the street, a car veered toward them. His attendant heard it and barely pushed them out of its path. It sped away, but Harold's helper was sure it was aiming for them."

"Cars swerve. Pedestrians get hit all the time. Is that it?"

"No. Someone knocked him over in the mall last week."

"Sounds like you should take this information to the police, not me."

"I did, but because I can't prove anything, they simply took my report." She stood and pushed the envelope closer to Burke. "If I wanted to learn the ins and outs of playing tennis or golf, I'd hire a pro. That's exactly what I'm doing now to fulfill Harold's bucket list."

"Not exactly." Burke could imagine a tennis or golf pro embracing her trim figure from behind while showing her how to swing through her shot. He doubted that came with his assignment.

"Maybe not with the same level of contact."

He recoiled, feeling she'd read his mind.

She laughed. "I think five hundred dollars for a retainer, plus your daily rate and expenses up to $5000 for two or three days of work is fair, don't you?"

"More than enough if I take your case, but this doesn't really seem like something up my alley. It feels like a game with me somehow being played as a patsy."

A line creased her forehead. "I assure you that's not the case."

Burke's hand again found its way back to his cigar. This time he picked it up and twirled it between his fingers.

"Why don't you light that up after I leave while you think about my offer? Personally, I feel certain that after a few calming puffs, you'll agree this is a win-win proposition for both of us. My number is on a card in the envelope."

Mrs. Taylor didn't wait for an answer. She headed toward the door.

He picked up the envelope. "Wait a minute. I need to give you a receipt for this."

She looked back over her shoulder. "Don't bother. I trust you. Hopefully, you'll trust me, too."

A grunt was the best he could do as a reply, but when she let the door close behind her, he assumed it satisfied her.

As he waited for his computer to power up, his hands immediately followed her direction to light up. Waiting for the start functions to end, Burke held his cigar above the flame of his torch lighter. He spun the cigar around to get an even burn. Rewarded with an orange glow, he popped it into his mouth and puffed rapidly, expelling smoke until its whiteness let him know the end was well lit. The process might not be as numbing as Taylor's wine, but he knew this habit would have satisfied Maggie as much as it did him.

Savoring the flavor of the cigar, Burke picked up the envelope. He trusted Mrs. Taylor enough not to count it. Dropping her card on his desk, he shoved the escaping bills and envelope into his desk drawer, next to his gun.

Pulling a legal pad on his desk toward him, he picked up a pen and drew a vertical line dividing the page into two columns he labeled "Yes" and "No." Under "Yes," he wrote "$3000–$5000." His "No" side, with "patsy, something rotten in Denmark, pretty gams, shiny diamond, and not fully believable," was longer.

Burke studied the two lists. He circled "Yes." Money and jobs had been scarce since Maggie's death and Dane's accusations. Maybe this job would turn things around for him.

After taking a long drag off his cigar, he decided the beach held too many memories for him, so he'd take Harold to the carousel first. Tapping his cigar out, he retrieved the card with her phone number.

She answered after the first ring.

"Mrs. Taylor, I've decided to take your case. I figure we'll start with the merry-go—"

She cut him off. "Good. Harold is up early, but usually naps in the late afternoon, so why don't we say I'll have him ready for you tomorrow at eight."

"I can make that work."

She hung up.

At exactly eight the next day, Burke stood outside the Taylor home. For comfort, he patted the cigars he'd put in his breast pocket and then rang the doorbell. Standing in front of the oak-paneled door, he imagined, from the house's size and the neighborhood, it had at least six bedrooms and eight baths. He fully expected a maid, but the door was opened by Mrs. Taylor.

Barefoot, she wore a ruffled white shirt and black denim pants. Her diamond earrings and pendant were each half the size of her ring. He assumed the stones decorating her jeans were rhinestones rather than diamonds, but then again.

"Come in." She stepped back from the door, so Burke could enter the two-story entry.

There was no question that his entire apartment could fit into it. A giant colored glass chandelier overhead caught his eye. He'd seen things like it before, but only in magazines or museums. He pointed to it. "That's quite a piece."

"On our honeymoon, Harold and I stumbled into a small shop in Murano. We fell in love with the glassblower's work. When we got home, we couldn't forget it, so Harold commissioned him to make one for us."

"And you shipped it here?"

"Yes. Once blown and put together, the fixture had to be disassembled, shipped, and reconstructed under the watchful eye of its creator."

"Sounds like an expensive project."

"Harold always says, 'What's money for if you don't spend it joyously?'"

Burke glanced at the chandelier and the art strategically hung in the entranceway. "Has it brought you happiness?"

She shrugged as she led him into a library that could have come out of a Dickens novel.

Her husband sat in a leather wingback chair. There was no attendant in sight.

Burke immediately recognized Taylor from his TV ads and, he realized, from some charity function Maggie dragged him to.

Taylor smiled at Burke. "Have we met?"

"No."

Mrs. Taylor laid her hand on her husband's shoulder. "Harold, this is Burke Williams. He's here to help you check off some of the items on your bucket list. Today, the two of you are going to visit the Flying Horse Carousel. You're going to have it all to yourself for at least an hour or two until it opens."

She bent and pecked Harold's head.

He glanced up at her and smiled. Harold turned to Burke. "Hello."

In the car, after glancing over to make sure Taylor's seat belt was fastened, Burke pulled away from the house. It was a short drive to Watch Hill. Not saying much to each other, they walked down still empty Bay Street toward the wood-framed pavilion that housed the carousel. Nearing the structure, Burke could see it was ten-sided with a hipped roof.

Hearing an intake of breath next to him, Burke turned to make sure his charge was okay. Taylor was staring at the carousel. Burke followed the direction of Taylor's gaze. The merry-go-round had about twenty gaily painted wood horses of two different sizes. Chains attached to the rump and an iron bar at the pommel of each horse suspended them from sweeps radiating out from below the canopy at the center of the carousel. "Do you want to wait around and take a ride?"

Taylor laughed and nodded toward a bench facing the merry-go-round. "I think we'd be better sitting over there and looking at it. You look a bit over the one-hundred-pound weight limit."

"I can stand next to you if you want to ride."

"Don't think that will work either. There's no floor to stand on. That's what, for the past hundred and twenty-five years or so, helped make this a unique attraction."

Burke glanced at the merry-go-round again. For someone who observed for a living, he'd missed that one. Maybe he'd been in the office too long.

Taylor continued staring at the carousel.

Burke didn't interrupt whatever Taylor was thinking about.

When Taylor finally spoke, his gaze didn't shift. "I'm sure you've heard how I bounced around between different foster homes. Some were good, some not. Making friends was difficult because I moved so much. When I was nine, I spent almost a year near here before I was shuttled off in the middle of the night. I always regretted not saying good-bye to the one friend I'd made. The moments she and I rode this carousel made the rest of my life bearable."

Taylor sighed, lost in his thoughts again.

"The carousel is built so that as it spins, the horses move away from the center making you feel like you're flying. From an outside horse, you have a chance to win another ride by grabbing a brass ring as you fly by it. I never had much luck, but my friend was successful almost every time. Because I had no money and she did, she always insisted I take the free ride."

"Sounds like a special friend." Burke assumed this was who Mrs. Taylor had mentioned.

"She was. A one in a million saint." Taylor reached into his pocket and pulled out a brass ring. He handed it to Burke.

Turning it over in his hand, Burke observed how scratched the brass was. "I never got to use that ring for a ride, but no matter where I moved, I kept it. I hoped if I found her again, I could propose with it."

"But you never found her?"

"I did." Taylor turned his head and met Burke's gaze. "She already was married."

"That must have been a gut kick."

"I could accept that. After all, I'd already been married once."

"So?"

"She married a bum." Taylor spoke faster. "I begged her to leave him, but she refused. I swore he'd hurt her. She disagreed. She believed he was redeemable and, more importantly, she loved him. When Maggie walked away, I promised that if you hurt her, you'd pay."

Burke recoiled. "My Maggie?"

Taylor nodded and grinned. "I may not remember where I put my keys or what I had for lunch but getting even for her is at the very top of my bucket list." He lunged at Burke, who pushed him away.

When Taylor didn't come after him again, Burke stood.

"I wouldn't do that. Sit down," Mrs. Taylor said.

Burke whipped his head toward her voice and stared at the gun in her gloved hand.

During his scuffle with Taylor, he hadn't heard her come up behind them. Had she been waiting on the far side of the carousel until this moment?

"Put your gun on the ground and kick it toward me. And don't get funny. I'm a fairly good shot."

He sat and complied.

Keeping her gun aimed at him, she squatted and picked up his gun.

"Why?" Burke asked.

"I told you I'd reached the point I needed to do something for both of us. Once I shoot you, the top item on Harold's bucket list will be checked off. His fingerprints will be on the gun, but with his dementia and a good lawyer, Harold will be institutionalized for the rest of his life. That will check off the only thing on my bucket list."

"But there was nothing between them?"

"Not physically, but Harold never gave up hoping. Do you know what it's like having three people in a marriage? Harold loved me, but he never stopped loving your wife more."

Burke felt the bullet slide by his cigars into his chest. As he slumped against the back of the bench, a red stain spreading across his chest, he saw the sparkle of Mrs. Taylor's diamond as she pressed her husband's hand around the gun's grip. His last thought was whether the new Boxed Wine Queen would raise a glass in his memory.

ZERO HOUR
by Josh Pachter

Building the time machine was the easy part. Once I figured out the math underlying the concept of quantum wave resurgence, the construction of a meatspace machine was child's play, took me two weeks of sixteen-hour days and less than four hundred dollars in materials.

The hard part was figuring out what to *do* with it, once I had it programmed and ready to rumble.

I've been fascinated pretty much all my life by the idea of time travel. One of my earliest memories is Yvette Mimieux in George Pal's 1960 film asking Rod Taylor in the far-off year 802,701 how the women of his time wear their hair—and then of course him rescuing her from the cannibalistic Morlocks, who gave me nightmares for months.

I was captivated when I discovered Jack Finney's marvelous *Time and Again*, which Stephen King has called "*the* great time-travel story"—then, decades later, captivated again by King's own *11/22/1963*.

On July 3, 1985, I stood on line for eight hours to make sure I got a front-row seat for the premiere of *Back to the Future*, and I lined up again on 11/22/1989 for the first public screening of *Part II* and yet again six months later for *Part III*. (And you can bet that on October 21, 2015, I showed up for work on "*Back to the Future* Day" in full Emmett Brown regalia: yellow jacket and trousers, red shirt, white fright wig, the whole nine yards.)

From Mark Twain's *A Connecticut Yankee in King Arthur's Court* to Audrey Niffenegger's *The Time Traveler's Wife* to Barb Goffman's recent *Crime Travel* anthology, I have read them all, and my DVD collection includes everything from *Godzilla vs. King Ghidorah* to *Frequency* to *Flight of the Navigator* and beyond. I've even got a VHS cassette of *The Jetsons Meet the Flintstones*, though it's been twenty years since I last had a VCR capable of playing it.

I have no idea why it took me so long to decide to build a time machine of my own. I suppose the idea that time travel might actually be *possible* was imprinted in my mind as science fictional, and I never really stopped to consider that it could be feasible IRL.

Until about six weeks ago, when I ran across a 2017 article by astrophysicist Ethan Siegel on the *Forbes* website. It was called "How Traveling Back in Time Could Really, Physically Be Possible," and that article changed my life. Well, changed *your* life, too, I guess. Changed *everyone's* life, in ways Dr. Siegel couldn't possibly have anticipated.

The trick, boiling it down to the simplest possible terms, was to generate a supermassive black hole and a negative mass/energy counterpart to it and then connect them to form a traversible wormhole into the past.

Like I said, child's play, once I wrestled my way through the math.

So there I was about ten o'clock this morning with what I knew was a fully functioning device, all dressed up with no place (or time) to go.

My first inclination was to set my Wayback Machine for the middle of the First Battle of Ypres in West Flanders, Belgium. I was particularly interested in one company on the German side, which entered the battle with two hundred and fifty soldiers and finished with only forty-two of them left alive. One of those forty-two was a twenty-five-year-old Austrian citizen who had requested and somehow been granted permission to serve in the Bavarian Army, and who at the time of the battle held the lowly rank of private and was assigned to serve as a regimental message runner.

Putting a bullet through Adolph Hitler's head would be too clichéd, though, I decided. Go back to pre-WWII Germany and put a bullet through Adolph Hitler's head...ho-hum.

I took four years of German in high school, though, and I've never used it for anything beyond a friendly "Gesundheit!" when someone sneezes, so I thought it would be nice to go somewhen that would allow me to put my rusty language skills to use. And I'd just finished reading Nabokov's *The Defense*, whose title character, Aleksandr Ivanovich Luzhin, was, according to the book's introduction, based on German chess master Curt von Bardeleben, who eked out a meager living marrying and divorcing wealthy women and ultimately threw himself or, according to one source, accidentally fell out a window on January 31, 1924, at the age of sixty-two.

What harm would it do, I figured, if a miserable old chess player shuffled off this mortal coil a day ahead of historical schedule?

After ten minutes of Internet research, I was able to dig up a home address for von Bardeleben. I set the time-and-place dials on my chariot, checked my watch against the old-fashioned round clock hanging on my basement wall—they agreed that it was 10:17 AM—strapped myself in and pressed the Engage button...and found myself in a musty sitting room in what, from the view of the Brandenburg Gate out the grimy window, I recognized must be a second- or third-floor apartment in Berlin.

I unbuckled and stepped out and looked around. The stink of boiled cabbage and potent cigars hung in the air. A door swung open, and in came a bearded gentleman in a tweed suit, carrying a cup of steaming coffee in his hand.

"Herr von Bardeleben?"

"*Ich bin* Curt von Bardeleben, *ja*," he said, his voice hoarse and cracked. "*Und wer, bitte, sind Sie?*"

I walked over to the window and opened it.

"*Ich bin dein Schicksal*," I replied. I am your Destiny.

And then I knocked the cup from his hand and flung him out into space. I watched him tumble Earthward—we were in fact on the *fourth* floor, I saw—and heard a dull thud as he smashed into the pavement below.

Then I returned to my time machine, climbed aboard and pressed the Recall button, blinked my eyes and found myself back in my basement.

I looked at my watch. It read 10:21 AM. According to the clock on the wall, though, it was still 10:17. I'd spent about four minutes in the past, and re-emerged from my temporal wormhole at the exact moment I'd left. Wait until Ethan Siegel heard about *this*.

I reset my watch to *here* time and looked around my makeshift lab. Everything seemed normal. I went upstairs and out the front door of my house, and my cul de sac was exactly the way it was supposed to be. The Sunday *Post* was in the driveway, and I scooped it up and brought it inside, made a pot of coffee and settled down to work the crossword.

I slid the paper out of its thin blue protective sleeve and unfolded it.

And there at the top of the front page, in a bold Gothic font, were the words *Tägliche Nachrichten.*

Oh, crap. I can practically recite Ray Bradbury's "The Sound of Thunder" by heart. How could I have forgotten the butterfly effect?

I had no idea how the slightly premature defenestration of an impoverished Berliner could have resulted in the *Washington Post* turning into a German-language newspaper, but what difference did the *how* of it make? The fact was, my act had changed the world in ways I had not anticipated, and it seemed likely that the changes were not for the better.

I was going to have to fix this, but—well, but *how*?

For the next quarter of an hour, I wracked my brains, and finally I decided, cliché or not, I'd have to either go big or go home. So I stuffed some supplies in my pockets, jury-rigged a ladder to the back of my makeshift Delorean, strapped myself in and set the dials.

I checked my watch against the clock on the wall: 10:42 AM. I pushed the button.

It was frigid on Calvary Hill. I hadn't expected it to be so cold— if I'd known, I'd've worn a parka and a pair of gloves. Three tall wooden crosses loomed against the night sky, illuminated only by the glow of the moon. The air was fresh and clean, but I could scent the slightest hint of iron on the chill breeze.

I unstrapped my ladder and carried it up Golgotha. The three young men hanging from the crosses, each of them naked except for a ragged loincloth, looked almost identical, but I was pretty sure the one I wanted was the one in the middle. I hoped so, since the other two—their legs twisted at impossible angles—were obviously already dead. I set my ladder against the middle cross and started upward.

The man hanging from the crossbar opened his eyes and spoke. I didn't recognize the language, and his voice was so hoarse I don't think I would have understood him even had he been speaking English. He seemed so close to gone, though, that I suppose he was probably saying something along the lines of "Father, into your hands I commend my spirit."

It wasn't easy, but with the help of the claw end of the hammer I fished from my pocket I managed to yank out the nail that spiked his feet to the cross's upright. Then I mounted another couple of steps and freed one of his hands from the crossbar, draped him over my right shoulder, and pulled the final nail from his other wrist.

I backed down the ladder and laid the poor son of a bitch on the ground. I'd brought mercurochrome and sterile gauze and bandages, and I cleaned and dressed his wounds as best I could. I had a bottle of water, too, and I tipped his head forward and gave him a drink. He must have been in incredible pain, but his dark eyes gazed up at me peacefully, and he murmured something I couldn't quite hear but took for thanks. His eyelids fluttered and closed, and I thought for a moment I'd arrived too late, but I pressed my fingertips to the side of his neck and felt a pulse, weak but steady.

A rumbling noise from below startled me. A woman who looked enough like the man I'd pulled down from the cross to be his mother was dragging a wheeled cart up the hill. She flung herself to the dirt by the young man's side and cradled him in her arms. I watched in awed silence as she comforted him, and then spotted a cloud of dust in the distance and realized a platoon of Roman soldiers was on its way.

I helped the woman load her son into the cart and rolled it carefully down the hill for her. Then she took over and hurried away, and as the sound of hoof beats thundered closer I loaded my bottle of antiseptic and leftover bandages and the empty water bottle and the hammer back into my pockets, quickly lashed the ladder to the stern of my machine, and pushed the Recall button and blinked my eyes.

I was back in my basement. I checked my watch: 11:38 AM. But the clock on the wall still read 10:42. I hadn't even been gone for a single minute.

I reset my watch and then, holding my breath in a combination of hope and fear, took the steps two at a time and raced into the kitchen, where I'd left the Sunday paper.

It was still the *Tägliche Nachrichten,* and the main above-the-fold headline read *"Donald Trump zieht US von den Vereinten Nationen zurück."* That was more complicated German than I had at my command, but I had a sneaking suspicion it meant that Ivanka's daddy was still the president and had withdrawn the United States from the UN. Holy smokes.

So rescuing Jesus hadn't put things back the way they was, goddammit. But had I once again made things *worse?* I didn't know.

With great trepidation, I crossed the living room and eased open the front door and took a look outside. Right across the street, where Dale and Mike used to live in a house the exact mirror image of my own, the golden dome of a mosque glittered in the sunshine. It was gorgeous, much more attractive than Dale and Mike's place. A PA system rigged at the top of its gleaming white minaret blared *"Ashhadu an la ilaha illa Allah,"* and a stream of sandaled men in long white thobes, their heads crowned with red-and-white-checked ghutras held in place by thin black agals, shuffled slowly through the open front door for morning prayers.

Don't get me wrong: I am not an Islamophobe. But if there was now a Muslim house of worship smack in the middle of my cul de sac, who *knew* what other *mishigas* I was responsible for?

I suddenly flashed on one of my favorite short stories, Alfred Bester's "The Men Who Murdered Mohammed," which I read long ago in a British anthology called, if memory serves, *Top Science Fiction*. "We're like millions of strands of spaghetti in the same pot," narrator Israel Lennox tells time traveler Henry Hassel. "When a man changes the past, he only affects his *own* past—no one else's."

Boy, oh, boy, did I have news for Israel Lennox.

In Bester's story, fine, it doesn't matter *what* you do, you only affect your own timeline, not the world's. But it turns out that, here in meatspace, it was Bradbury who had it right, and every action really *does* affect everything else. Every change made to the past changes the present, and continued changes to the past, whether they're deeper *in* the past or closer *to* the present, make accumulated changes in the *here* and *now*.

So how in the Germanized-thanks-to-me, Muslimized-thanks-to-me world was I supposed to fix this?

It didn't take me long to figure it out. The only way to put things back the way they were supposed to be would be to undo my ever having used my time machine in the first place.

I looked around my house, at my bookshelves filled with novels and short-story collections and old pulp magazines, at my DVDs, at the posters on the walls advertising *Looper* and *12 Monkeys*, *Bill & Ted's Excellent Adventure* and *Groundhog Day*, and heaved a heartfelt sigh. I would miss all this.

What I was about to do would take more courage than I felt able to muster without assistance, so I went into the kitchen and got an unopened bottle of sangria from the fridge. I peeled an orange and cut it into small pieces, sliced a banana, and was dicing an apple when I realized I was stalling. Leaving the fruit on the counter, I raised my glass and toasted the Great Unknown and tossed the wine down the hatch in a single gulp.

Feeling about a thousand years old, I trudged back down to the basement and picked up my 1903 Browning and made sure it was still loaded and slipped it into my pocket.

I settled myself in my machine and looked at my watch and the clock on the wall. They agreed that it was 10:59 AM.

I set the dials for today's date, two hours in the past.

I pushed the button.

And there I was, my back to me, hunched over my Macbook Pro, putting the finishing touches on my program.

I eased silently out of the time machine and pulled the gun from my pocket. My hand was shaking.

I glanced at the clock on the wall: zero hour, 9:00 AM.

I swallowed and took a deep breath.

"Hello, Darkness, my old friend," I whispered.

At the sound of my voice, I looked up from my keyboard and turned around in my chair. My brows were furrowed in surprise.

I took careful aim and, before I could do anything to stop me, pulled the trigg

DAS ENDE

CHIMERA
by Libby Hall

"Hey Ivy! You hear they found Big Jed Powell dead in Sayers Junkyard?" Lee Dory asked me while I was wiping glasses. "I heard his head looked like a busted up watermelon."

The news was three days old, so I'd already heard it from a dozen other people. When you work in a small-town bar most of what you hear is crap, but when you hear one thing and then another, you start to get a picture of what's really happening. So as usual, I was taking it all in.

I shrugged and jerked my head down the bar to where Hollis Sims, my boyfriend and the town Sheriff, was hunched over a glass of Maker's (three fingers, straight). He stopped in sometimes to get information, but usually just to unwind after a long day. For the most part people left him alone. The fact that Hollis had just ordered Maker's instead of his usual Beam told me he'd been at the scene again.

"You might want to keep it down," I said to Lee. "Hollis has had a bad week."

Lee glanced at Hollis and shrugged. He had already drunk four beers since knocking off from his construction job, and God knows how many in the truck on the way to the bar. Slim chance he was gonna tone down the volume.

"Well, nobody'll be sad to see that SOB gone," he said, his voice carrying across the room. "The trick'll be to figure out who did it. Half this town would give their eyeteeth to see Big Jed pushin' daisies. I heard they already hauled Jemma and Ricky down for questions."

I always felt sorry for Jemma Powell, Big Jed's wife. Back in the day, I heard Big Jed could be charming when he wanted to be, wearing a leather jacket and riding his fixed-up Indian motorcycle instead of a truck like the rest of the boys. Story was that Jemma came home from a date with Jed looking like she'd been doing more than holding hands, and those brothers of hers tracked Jed out by the lake and beat the snot out of him. Jemma and Big Jed broke up for a while after that, but later on he got Jemma pregnant. She moved in with him and had Ricky when she was seventeen. For a while she seemed happy. She'd be walking around town, doing errands and talking to people. Folks even thought maybe being a daddy would settle Big Jed down, but Jemma looked old and tired by the time she had her second son, Bobby. She must have been around nineteen. I was young, so it was a long time before I clued in to why she wore sunglasses on a rainy day, and hardly ever wore short sleeves.

I'm not saying Jemma killed him, but you never know.

I've worked at the Green Door for a long time and my best friend's a social worker, so I've picked up a thing or two. First, people's drinks reflect who they are, or sometimes who they're trying to be; second, people who get bullied their whole lives don't seem to know how to not be bullied. Jemma's a prime example. Sure, some people break that mold, but seems like most just keep coming back for more. When they come in here, I serve them drinks so they can forget, or maybe to get the courage to fight back.

Hollis glanced up at Lee but didn't say anything. I reached back and started pulling another beer for Lee. Sucking on that might keep him quiet until I could convince him to leave.

"You know it ain't nice to talk ill of the dead," I said.

Lee flushed and raised his voice even louder. "Well I know him and Ricky shot Old Man Porter's dog Daisy just for crossing onto their property and scaring the turkeys they was shooting. Ain't no reason for shooting a dog. It don't know where those property lines are. I thought Old Man Porter was gonna have a heart attack." I glanced up and saw Lee was actually getting teary-eyed. It was definitely time for him to go.

He looked over at Hollis and bellowed, "I hope there ain't no evidence lying around; sometimes you just got to let sleeping dogs lie."

Hollis sighed. "You want to make an official complaint?" he asked Lee.

Lee shook his head. "Hell no. Those two sum-bitches would come after me faster than grass through a goose."

"That's what I thought," Hollis said. He sighed, left some cash on the bar and left.

"I'm calling your wife, Lee," I said. "Again."

Lee narrowed his eyes and stared at me like he was going to pick a fight, which we've done before. He's lost every time. I'm stronger than I look and dating a cop means I know holds that are pretty useful. After a couple of seconds, he looked down and dug around in his pocket.

By the time Lee left, the bar was getting busy as more folks got off work. Big Jed's murder was the talk of the town, and my customers were spouting theories on who did it, ranging from Jemma to his waste-of-space oldest son Ricky, or one of his druggie customers. Even shy, skinny Bobby, his younger son, got a few votes. But mostly people thought Ricky did it.

*

The paper didn't mention a weapon, and since Big Jed was killed in Carl Sayers' old car junkyard, it could've been a tire iron or a thousand other pieces of junk. The paper did say there was a case of cheap beer cans and a bunch of cigarettes nearby (Ricky and Big Jed's brands). Of course, half the county drank and smoked the same things, so I didn't really see it as compelling evidence. They must have found something more concrete, but if they did, the paper wasn't saying. Big Jed was a mechanic, and I imagine he spent a lot of time wandering around Sayers—it wouldn't have taken Sherlock Holmes to track him and jump him back where nobody could see. God knows how long it will take Hollis to find the murder weapon, if it's even still there.

Lee was right—they were going to have a hard time figuring out who did it unless there was some real evidence left behind. Personally, I hoped it was Jemma, but my money was on Ricky. Even when they were kids, if Bobby was getting bullied too bad Ricky would take down whoever it was. Ricky had a soft spot for his little brother when he wasn't beating the crap out of Bobby himself. Ricky and Big Jed went at it pretty often, too, judging by the number of times they've both shown up in town sporting black eyes and split lips.

Ricky has always been a piece of work, fighting, stealing, and just generally being your small-town badass. Bobby was a smart, nerdy kid who was bullied at home and in school, who grew up to be a soft-spoken, nerdy pharmacist that got bullied everywhere else. His girlfriend Shay was like Bobby, a shy, local girl who hardly looked anybody in the eye.

But a week earlier, I'd been surprised to see Bobby Powell and Shay arguing with Big Jed outside the bar in the morning.

"I told you, I want my money," Big Jed was saying, standing toe-to-toe to Bobby. Shay was standing behind Bobby, looking white as a sheet. That wasn't surprising. Shay likes her weed and, according to Hollis, Big Jed had his hands in every drug deal in the county. Bobby stood with his fists clenched, chin jutting out in perfect presentation to receive a punch.

Someone has got to teach that boy how to fight, I thought.

"And I told you, you'd have it when I get paid again," Bobby said.

Shay put her hand on Bobby's arm, trying to pull him away. "C'mon Bobby, he knows what's up. He's just making his point."

Bobby shook her off, his eyes never leaving his daddy. Big Jed shoved Bobby back a step. "Maybe I'll just take what you owe me another way," he growled, and looked at Shay. I've seen that look before, and it usually ends up with me thrashing some asshole that thinks all women are scared of them. Shay definitely looked scared. I took a step around the bar just in case.

Big Jed took a step closer to Shay, I think just to see what Bobby would do.

"You think she'd scream like your mama does, son?" he asked Bobby.

Bobby roared and took an awkward swing at Big Jed. It was a

weak blow that barely glanced off his chin.

"Don't you ever threaten her!"

Big Jed and Shay both stared at Bobby with surprise. Then Big Jed started to laugh.

Bobby turned beet red but stood his ground. Shay grabbed him and steered him to their pickup.

"You'll get your money, Mr. Powell," Shay called, shoving Bobby at the truck and climbing into the front seat. She peeled out of the parking lot and I sighed with relief. Crisis averted.

If Hollis had asked, I'd have told him about Bobby and Shay's argument with Big Jed, but if I told him everything I heard in here, half the town would be behind bars or suspects of one thing or another. Hollis doesn't ask and I don't offer unless it's important. So far, we've been able to make that work pretty well.

*

After Lee left, my best friend Maggie Jones came in looking discouraged, as usual. Like all social workers, she has too many families to take care of and not enough funding or time to do it. There are more lines around her eyes than someone just shy of forty should have. Plenty of kids running around town should thank their lucky stars Maggie intervened. I'm pretty sure no one but me knows about the hours she spends writing reports, trying to get them the help they need.

I slid her usual vodka tonic over as she took her stool. "So, what's the rumor mill saying today?" she asked.

"Let's see…Lee Dory mentioned Sandy Sherman before he got obnoxious and chased Hollis out. I've heard a couple of other stories about people Big Jed's done wrong, but nothing out of the ordinary for him. What about you?"

Maggie sighed and sipped her drink. "Hell, Ivy, seems like everybody's got a reason to hate him. He was a thug and half the town was scared of what him and Ricky'd do to them." She sat back. "But I just heard Ricky's been in and out of the hospital again. Seems his remission glory days are over. The cancer's back, and apparently he isn't doing well."

I poured her another vodka tonic, this one much weaker since I knew Maggie was driving. "Well, it looks like Ricky'll get what's coming to him, but I don't know how Bobby would have survived without you."

Maggie sighed. "At least that is one solid victory I can take credit for. Thank God he got to do that pharmacy program. I don't know where he'd be right now."

"Working the night shift at the chicken plant and being a punching bag, if Big Jed had anything to do with it."

A few years ago, Maggie, in a moment of pure brilliance, had told Big Jed that Bobby would end up taking care of him really good if he played his cards right. Chemistry is a good thing to know when you're thinking about setting up an "alternative medicine" distribution company. A week later Big Jed signed the permission forms.

It was too bad Ricky never had the focus to do something like that. Instead, he followed his roots and terrorized the town like his old man.

Carol Ann Pugh, one of the nurses at St. Theresa's and a Tequila Sunrise kind of girl, overheard Maggie and said, "Sometimes when people get cancer it makes them more appreciative, and sometimes it makes them sad or mad, but I've never seen it make a body hateful. Ricky Powell actually spit on me one time when I was trying to clean his chemo port. I still can't believe that baby brother of his bothered to donate bone marrow to that pile of shit."

"Bobby did? Why?"

Carol Ann tossed back her long, bottle-red hair and shrugged. "I don't know. One day he wandered in and said he wanted to see if he was a match. When he was, he just scheduled a time to come in, did it, and left."

See what I mean? The stuff people will tell me after a drink or two? You might as well not sign HIPAA papers. I know more about the weird stuff that's happening to people in this town than Jesus does, probably, if it came down to confessions.

As the night was winding down, Bobby Powell showed up looking shell-shocked. It was the first time he'd been in the bar since the murder. He usually comes in alone after work and seems happy to sit for a while, just sipping one Eagle Rare straight up because he can afford it. He never causes any issues.

He quietly slipped onto a stool, and I poured him his usual.

"I'm sorry about your daddy," I said softly as I slid it over to him. He nodded, but he didn't say anything. He took a sip, put the glass down again and stared at his hands.

I was surprised he showed up, what with all the attention he'd get, but Bobby probably needed to drown his sorrows in here as much as anyone else would. Plus, in a small town, the more you hide the more people want to know why you're hiding. After about twenty minutes he finished his drink, paid the tab and shuffled out to the parking lot.

Carol Ann Pugh pushed her way back to the bar and plunked herself onto Bobby's empty stool. Her tank top revealed a rainbow tattoo on her enormous chest. Thank God she had to wear scrubs at work—she'd cause strokes just leaning over. Carol Ann ordered a light beer "to balance a basket of fries," she said, as if that was going to make a difference.

"Bobby looks like he's actually upset."

"Maybe it's because it's his daddy that got killed," I said, rolling my eyes.

She leaned across the bar and whispered, "They took a DNA sample from Ricky yesterday."

"They did? Why?" Like everybody else, I figured Ricky would have been too weak from the cancer to do much of anything, much less bust up his old man. I guess they have to cover their bases.

"Well, I guess it's because they think he did it, Ivy," Carol Ann said, looking at me as if I had brain damage. "Gawd, try to keep up." She took another swallow before hoisting herself off the stool and wandering back to the pool table.

*

Two days later, Hollis knocked on the bar door in the morning while I was cleaning and getting ready to open. I let him in, and he climbed on the stool at the end of the bar where no one could see him from the sidewalk.

"Why do you look like the cat that swallowed the canary?" I asked.

"We arrested Ricky and Bobby Powell last night," he said, "but I let Bobby go. Looks like Ricky will finally start paying for some of his sins."

"I heard y'all took a DNA sample from him."

He nodded. "Had to. The blood at the junkyard came up as Ricky's, Big Jed's and Bobby."

"Wait, Bobby? Skinny little Bobby was there too?"

Hollis was quiet for a second, then he shrugged. "Turns out, when we did the DNA testing on Ricky, he's what they call a chimera."

"What the hell is a chimera?" I asked.

"Two DNA strands besides Big Jed's showed up in the blood we got from the scene. According to the lab, the only way that can happen is if there were three people there, or if there's been a bone marrow transplant. Apparently, sometime after the marrow donation, the recipient's blood, in this case Ricky's, can show up as having both the recipient's and the donor's DNA, or even just the donors. It's called being a chimera."

I was trying to follow, and Hollis waited for me to start putting the pieces together. "So, when you tested Ricky's DNA, both his and Bobby's DNA came up?"

Hollis nodded. "We brought Bobby in, but he wasn't talking and said he wanted a lawyer. While he was waiting for that to happen, I went to get Ricky, but he was in the hospital. He'd checked himself in and looked like he already had one foot out the door. I didn't know he was that sick. Anyway, I told him I'd arrested his brother for killing Big Jed, and now it was his turn because both their DNA was all over the place. Ricky was quiet for a minute, and then he said, 'Bobby weren't there. It was all me. You better get the cuffs on me before I die on you, too.'"

"So, you didn't have to arrest Bobby after all?"

Hollis shook his head. "Nope. We got Ricky's confession. The DA said that's all we need." He looked hard at me. "Do you know of any reason I should talk to Bobby?" he asked.

I remembered all those times growing up and seeing Jemma walking around town in long sleeves, or Maggie telling me how Bobby showed up at school sporting bruises he said came from riding his dirt bike. I thought about Big Jed threatening to do something to Shay and the fact that Bobby came in the bar alone this last time. I guessed Shay had left him. Having Big Jed in her life would have been pretty terrifying.

"Nope. I can't think of anything," I said.

Hollis reached into his pocket and slid a brown paper lunch bag across the bar. "I also found this at the junkyard, but I forgot about it until this morning."

Inside the bag was an empty pint-sized bottle of Eagle Rare.

"Not a lot of people around here drink that," I said carefully.

Hollis said. "It must've fallen out of one of those old cars." He looked at me for a long, few seconds. "You should probably just throw it away. We got the right man."

Hollis eased off the stool and headed for the door. He called back over his shoulder as he left, "You tell Bobby the next drink is on me."

OUT OF COMMISSION
by Heather Weidner

Delanie Fitzgerald tuned out the chatter from her friends at the paint party and stared at what was supposed to be a lighthouse. She tilted the canvas, but the look didn't improve. The monolith still resembled the Leaning Tower of Pisa.

"Pass the blue, and I probably need more of that pink punch, too," her friend, Paisley Ford said as she reached for a larger brush.

Kristi Bell, the owner of Paint the Town, slid the containers toward Paisley and refilled everyone's glasses.

"Looking good, ladies." Kristi flitted around her cozy shop, dispensing advice. "Your lighthouse looks like the one in Cape Hatteras. Delanie, you doing okay over there?"

"I'm not sure this is my thing, but I'm always up for an adventure," Delanie said.

Robin Kirby looked up from her beach scene and white lighthouse. "Speaking of adventures, Delanie, how's work? What's the girl P.I. been up to lately?"

"It's been busy with some insurance fraud and cheating spouse cases." Delanie eyed her lighthouse and added some more black.

"What exactly do you do?" Kristi interrupted, setting more paint containers on the table.

"She owns Falcon Investigations." Paisley added white highlights.

"That must be interesting." Kristi's voice trailed off.

"Some days. A lot of the time, it's hours of boring stakeouts, but we usually get the bad guy."

Kristi nodded. "It looks like you all are wrapping up. Take your time and let me know if you need anything. There are plenty more snacks and pink punch."

*

The next morning during breakfast, Delanie's phone buzzed.

She fished it out of her bag. "Falcon Investigations."

"Hi, Delanie. This is Kristi Bell from Paint the Town. I'd like to talk to you about a job."

"Oh, hi. What can we help you with?"

"Can we meet? Is ten okay? At my shop?"

"That works. See you then." Delanie disconnected and dialed her partner, Duncan Reynolds, who did web design when he wasn't using his hacking skills to find information in the dark corners of the internet. When she got his quirky voicemail, she said, "Hey. We have a potential new client. I'll call ya later."

Delanie pulled into one of the empty spots in front of Paint the Town and grabbed her briefcase. Tiny bells tinkled when she pushed the door open. Not seeing anyone inside, she yelled, "Kristi, it's Delanie."

"I'm back here. There's coffee on the counter. Help yourself. Be right out."

Delanie poured coffee into a mug, and by the time she'd put in enough creamer to turn it tan, Kristi came through the door carrying a plastic bin. "Thanks for seeing me on short notice. Have a seat."

Delanie chose a lavender wooden chair, and Kristi continued, "You sparked something last night when you said you were a P.I. I had to call you before I lost my nerve. My sister disappeared last year. Weeks went by without any word, and then they found her body near a river." She took a breath and wiped her eyes with the back of her hand. "I'm sorry. The police haven't made an arrest yet. And I don't think anybody's working on the case. It's been so long since we've heard anything. I was hoping you could help me." She pulled a thick folder from the bin and dropped it on the table.

"I'm so sorry for your loss. "My partner and I can look into this for you."

Kristi tapped the thick folder. "This has copies of the police report. Everybody thought Liz and her husband Dan had the perfect marriage. But Dan claimed Liz was having an affair. I know it's been a year since she disappeared, but I'm hoping you can uncover what really happened to her."

"Tell me more about her husband." Delanie grabbed a pen and pad from her purse to take notes.

"My parents got a call from Dan that Liz never came back after dinner out. Weeks later, some teens found her body by a river in a secluded neighborhood."

"We'll see what we can find." Delanie handed her a contract and information sheet.

Kristi skimmed the documents and signed the last page. Afterward, she jotted a number on the back of a business card and handed it to Delanie. "This is my cell. Call anytime."

About a half hour later, Delanie parked in front of her office and let herself in. "Duncan?"

"Back here," he yelled.

"I brought food."

"Anything for Margaret?"

"I wouldn't forget your sidekick." Delanie set her purse, two bags, and a drink carrier on the conference room table. Duncan wandered in and grabbed a bag. A few moments later, his English bulldog Margaret, a brown and white log with legs, waddled in and took up residence under the table. Duncan ripped a cheeseburger into small pieces and put them on the wrapper on the floor. Margaret wasted no time wolfing it down.

"Our new client's sister disappeared about a year ago. She wants us to warm up the cold case."

"Got any details?" He rose and returned a few seconds later with his laptop and plopped down in a chair.

"Here's what the family got from the police." She handed him the folder. "Liz Harper left one night for dinner and never returned. Teens found her several weeks later near the Appomattox River. I'm going to see the property this afternoon. Her sister said the husband suspected Liz of having an affair."

Duncan raised his eyebrows and tapped away on his laptop.

"I'll see what's in the police report and work up a profile on the Harpers."

After driving to the other side of Chesterfield County, Delanie pulled into the Twelve Oaks neighborhood and cruised until she found the address that matched the police report. A For Sale sign with a picture of a smiling real estate agent stood sentry in the front yard. Parking in front of the brick McMansion, she dialed the number on the sign to listen to the house's amenities.

Delanie circled the house. A huge brick patio with a built-in hot tub dominated the flat part of the backyard. The rest sloped down to the river. Delanie walked the edge of the embankment, covered with entangled branches and underbrush. She snapped a few pictures. When she turned to get a picture of the backyard, she noticed a figure near the house. The man moved toward her.

He swung his arms around as he wobbled down the hill. When the pudgy figure got closer, he stopped to catch his breath. "Excuse me. Can I help you? You're on private property," he sputtered.

"Oh, hi." Delanie turned on her most charming smile. "I'm Elise Greene, a personal assistant, and my employer is looking for a new home. I thought I'd look around when I saw the sign."

He cleared his throat and stood up straight. "Well, hello. I'm Stephen Charles." He thrust his hand out. Her memory flicked back to the smiling photo on the real estate sign.

"The house is beautiful. My employer wants a property with a lot of space. He's looking for what he calls 'his sanctuary.'"

"Then this is the home for him. Does he have an agent?" he asked, still clutching her hand.

Delanie shook her head, and he guided her back to the front of the house and blathered on about the chef's kitchen and basement suite.

On the front porch, he punched some numbers in his phone for the lockbox. He popped out the key and opened the door. "This way, please."

Stephen directed her through the foyer, to an open den/kitchen.

"Your boss will love the view. The windows on this side catch the morning sun. The neighboring property over there is part of the historic Eppington property."

"What's Eppington?" Delanie asked.

"It's a lovely plantation once owned by Francis Eppes, Thomas Jefferson's wife's cousin. When Jefferson was the French ambassador, two of his daughters stayed there. One of the daughters is buried on the property."

Delanie smiled, and he continued with the tour. He prattled on about the luxurious floor plan and the extraordinary value of the house.

When they returned to the kitchen, Stephen asked, "When can we get together with your boss?"

"Mikko only wants to tour the top three properties on my list."

"How does this house compare?" Stephen stared at her.

"Good. So far. Could I see the basement?"

"This way. What do you and Mikko do exactly?" Stephen descended the stairs.

"He owns a cybersecurity company." Delanie wandered around the huge, empty space. She opened the door and did a quick scan of the backyard. "Lots of space down here. Hey, wasn't this the house where they found a dead body a year or so ago?"

A frown darkened his face. "Uh, no. Not in this house. You must be confused." He stared at her while clenching both of his hands.

Delanie moved around the room. "Are you sure about the murder? Something about it popped up when I Googled this address. I'm sure it was in this neighborhood."

"No, you're wrong," he said, raising his voice. His body tensed.

"I saw an article about it. Here, let me find it." Delanie pulled out her phone.

As Delanie scrolled through Google, Stephen made a noise that sounded like a growl from a feral animal. He lowered his head and rushed toward her. Grabbing her arm, he twisted it behind her back.

Wiggling out of his wrestler-like grip, she kicked him in the groin. She smacked his head with the closet door, and he dropped to the floor in a fetal position. Not finding anything she could use as a weapon, she stepped on his neck with her boot. "Stay down," she said. "What do you think you're doing? Are you nuts?" She took a deep breath and tried to look as menacing as possible. Why did this guy flip out after just a few questions?

"It wasn't supposed to be like this," he sobbed into the carpet.

"Keep your hands where I can see them." She tapped on her phone.

"Don't call the cops," he sniffed. "Let me explain. I am under so much stress. I got this listing—my first big one ever. And I can't sell it. I've spent thousands on the advertising and catered open houses, but nobody's interested. The market's flat. I freaked out when you asked about the dead woman."

"Keep talking." Delanie kept her foot on his neck.

"About a year ago, a realtor wanted to do a showing. Then she called back and said her lockbox wasn't working. Excited that we finally had some interest, I rushed over and let them in. I came back later to make sure all the lights were off and the doors were locked. I check on this place a lot."

"Is there a point to this?"

"I'm getting to it. I found something in the basement." He paused and sniffed.

"Go on." Delanie added pressure with her foot.

"There was a dead woman in the closet," he whispered.

"And you called the police?"

"Uh, no. She was already dead. I couldn't have the stigma of a murder on this listing. It's hard enough to sell already. I panicked. That night, I carried her outside and pushed her down the hill. They found her, and my listing wasn't involved. It all worked out."

"You destroyed a crime scene. What do you think the police would say? And how do I know you didn't kill her?"

"I had nothing to do with it. I swear," he whined. "I was afraid that I'd get blamed for it since I was on record for opening the house that day. The police only called once to let me know about the body. You gotta believe me. It could happen to anyone."

"Hardly. Did you know the dead woman?"

"No. She came with the other realtor, uh Bev Russell, who showed the house."

"Did you tell Bev about what you found?"

"No." Stephen sobbed louder. "I was okay when no one mentioned it. And I wasn't a hundred percent sure it was Bev's client. One of the back doors had been left unlocked."

Delanie headed for the stairs. He raised his head and asked, "Do you think Mikko will still be interested in the house?"

"Doubtful. But you better answer my calls if I have any more questions." Delanie didn't wait for his reply.

When she was safely inside her black Mustang with the doors locked, she called Duncan.

"Hey, what's up?"

"Could you look up Bev Russell? I think I need to pay her a visit."

Thirty minutes later, Delanie hip-checked the car's door and let herself into the office. "Duncan…"

"Coming," he yelled.

"What did you uncover?"

"Bev Russell is a big shot with Chalmers Realty. She sells a lot of high-end properties. The Harpers had been married for sixteen years. Flashy cars, big house, and lots of debt. Here are some photos I found online."

"I met the listing agent. He weirded out and jumped me when I asked about the murder."

"You okay?"

"Yep. I had to remind him of his manners. He said he can't sell the property, and he's into it for thousands in advertising. When he found a dead woman in the basement, he dragged the body down to the river. He was afraid that the murder would stain the property listing."

"Caring sort." Duncan tapped on his keyboard.

"I'm going to check out Bev Russell." Delanie grabbed her burner phone from her purse and punched in the realtor's number.

"Chalmers Realty. It's a beautiful day for homeownership. How may I help you?"

"Is Bev Russell available?"

"Let me check for you," the perky voice said.

After a long pause, Delanie heard, "Hello, this is Bev Russell."

"Hi. I'm Elise Greene. A client recommended you, and I was hoping to talk with you about some properties."

"I have some time this afternoon. How about three thirty?"

"I appreciate you squeezing me in."

"If you'll give me some idea of what you're looking for, I can do some research before you get here."

"It's for my boss, Mikko Morales. He wants at least six bedrooms, a gourmet kitchen, and space for a game room."

"What's his price range?"

"Right now, his max is two million."

There was a pause on the other end. Bev quickly recovered. "There are several nice properties on the market in that price range. I'll have some choices for you when I see you this afternoon."

"Thank you." Delanie pushed the red button to disconnect.

Duncan smiled. "I put Mikko and Elise on social media in case anyone checks."

Five minutes before her appointment with Bev Russell, Delanie pulled into the parking lot. She turned on the hidden camera in her purse. The smiling receptionist welcomed her with a wave.

"I'm Elise Greene. I'm here to see Bev Russell."

"I'll let her know you're here. Can I get you a drink?"

"No thanks." Delanie dropped into an oversized chair. She

flipped through emails on her phone until a blond approached.

"I'm Bev Russell."

"It's nice to meet you." Delanie rose and shook the woman's outstretched hand.

"Let's go to the conference room. We'll be more comfortable there." Bev pointed down the hall. "There are eight properties that fit your criteria. Here are the printouts." Bev tapped on her laptop and the homes appeared on the large TV mounted to the wall.

Delanie watched drone-filmed videos without comment.

When the last one ended, Bev asked, "Well, what do you think?"

"These are all lovely. I'd like to see the first one and the fifth one. There's also another one I'd like to ask you about. Mikko saw one in the Twelve Oaks neighborhood that caught his attention. That wasn't in the ones you showed me. Is it still available?"

She tapped her phone. "I don't see one in that price range there. Is he specifically interested in Chesterfield?"

"No. But he fell in love with that house. It's all he could talk about after he saw all those windows." Delanie turned on the charm with her best toothy smile.

"I need you to get him to sign this representation agreement. Can you fax it to me today? We'll also need to get a financial preapproval for Mikko as soon as possible."

Bev tapped on her computer keyboard. "Uh, I don't see the one in Twelve Oaks. But these other ones are fabulous. Do you want me to set up some showings?" Delanie nodded, and Bev continued, "Here is a buyer's packet. Call me if you have any questions. I look forward to working with you and Mikko. See you soon." Bev's smile reminded Delanie of the Cheshire cat in a designer suit.

Delanie drove down the block and parked where she could see the front door of the realty company. While she waited, she scoured Kristi's folder again. On a page stuck between two other police reports, she found a name and phone number for a Ben Zello scrawled in the margin. No other mention of him. Delanie texted Duncan to see if he could find anything on Zello.

She was getting restless about twenty minutes later when her phone played Duncan's ring tone.

"Hey, I found your Zello guy. He's a plumber in Midlothian."

"Any connection to the Harpers?"

"Not that I can find. I'll text you his info." Duncan disconnected.

Delanie pulled out her burner phone and called the number.

"Blue Dog Plumbing," a southern voice drawled.

"Hi, this is Ellen Smith. Is Ben Zello available?"

"He's wrapping up a job. I expect him back here around five."

"Thanks." Delanie drove to the office, an end unit at an older strip mall, that looked empty. Delanie found an inconspicuous spot to wait behind the building. Around a quarter to six, a blue Explorer parked next to the dumpster. Delanie compared the driver to the picture Duncan sent. A match.

Ben Zello climbed out of his SUV. She drove closer and pulled up beside him. "Mr. Zello?" He turned and she continued. "I'm Ellen Smith. Do you have a minute or two to answer some questions?"

"Uh, I guess. If it doesn't take long."

"I'm doing a story on Liz Harper, and I wanted to know how you knew her."

"Liz Harper? Name's not ringing a bell. I do a lot of jobs around here." He pulled out his phone and flipped through his contacts. "Harper. I did a bathroom reno for a Dan Harper once. Any kin?"

"Liz was his wife."

"I might have met her. I can't put a face to the name."

Delanie found Liz's picture and held it up for him. "This help?"

"No, sorry." The tall guy shook his head. "Nope."

"Thanks for your time." Another impasse. The leads in this case were frozen solid.

Delanie drove back to the realty company and parked near the entrance. Maybe she could find something by watching Bev Russell.

About six thirty, the realtor exited the office. Delanie let Bev get a car length ahead of her and then followed the black Mercedes to a historic tavern near the county line. A few minutes later, a silver Tesla with gullwing doors parked next to the Mercedes. Bev climbed out of her car and hugged the other driver. After a prolonged squeeze, they entered the tavern.

Delanie dialed Duncan. "Hey. I'm still out snooping. Could you look up a plate for me? It's a silver Tesla with a personalized Virginia plate, COOL HUH."

When the clicking sound from his keyboard stopped, he said, "Yes, it's cool. And it belongs to Dan Harper."

"Are you serious?" Delanie's pulse quickened. "I'm going to sit tight and see where they go next."

Delanie hated stakeouts. The private investigator squirmed in her seat to ward off the kinks. She jumped when the pair exited the tavern hand-in-hand.

Delanie followed Bev who trailed Dan Harper's car. They wended their way through backroads to a huge home in the Bexley neighborhood. Delanie parked in front of the neighbor's house and watched Dan pull in the garage. Bev parked in the driveway and followed him inside. A light went on downstairs, and a few minutes later, another one could be seen upstairs. A bored Delanie turned off the camera and headed for the nearest drive-thru for a late dinner.

Finishing her salad at her kitchen table that doubled as a home office, Delanie flipped through the pages Bev gave her. Pulling out her burner phone, she punched in Bev's number.

Delanie wondered if she was interrupting anything. When Bev answered, she said, "This is Elise Greene. I talked with Mikko, and he's really interested in the two properties we talked about."

"Very good. When would you like to see them?"

"Tomorrow?" Delanie twirled her pen, waiting for a response.

"How about one o'clock? I'll set up the showings and call you with the details."

"That's great. One more thing. Mikko wants me to look at another house. The MLS number is 1732832," Delanie said.

"Let me get a pen." After some shuffling sounds, Bev said, "Give it to me again."

Delanie repeated the number.

"I'll add it to the list."

*

The next morning, Delanie's burner phone vibrated on the table.

"Hi, this is Bev. I've scheduled all three showings for this afternoon. We'll start at the house in Twelve Oaks."

"Great. I'll meet you at that address."

"I'll see you at one." Bev clicked off.

Delanie pulled into the driveway a few minutes ahead of her appointment and waited for the realtor. Ten minutes later, a black car roared into the driveway and screeched to a stop next to Delanie's Mustang.

"This is the first stop on our tour," Bev said. "It's a handsome home with a great view. Let's go see what else it has."

"Yes. This is Mikko's favorite." Delanie waited for Bev to punch in her lockbox code.

"This way." Bev escorted Delanie through the foyer that resembled a medieval cathedral. "This is the fabulous first floor. Great for entertaining."

"Perfect. Mikko wants a game room. And he loves to entertain."

Bev nodded and led her around as she blabbed on about all the amenities. Without pausing to take a breath, she opened the basement door.

"Bev, this house is magnificent. Can you tell me any of its history?" Delanie asked, descending the steps.

"It's been vacant for about a year now. The owners had to relocate. If your boss is interested, I'm pretty sure the seller is ready to make a deal." She followed Delanie downstairs.

"I saw online that a murder occurred near here. Did the victim live here?"

Bev, distracted by her phone, tapped something into the screen.

"Oh, sorry. I had a text. That's the first I've heard of a murder nearby. Are you sure it was this neighborhood?"

"Here's the news article I found."

The realtor tapped something in her phone and stepped over to see Delanie's screen.

After she finished skimming the article, she said, "I wouldn't worry about it. That says someone died down by the river. I'm sure it had nothing to do with this place," she said with a smirk.

Delanie stepped outside and looked at the backyard. Then she walked around the cavernous basement. Her footsteps echoed in the empty rooms. Her head turned when she heard a noise upstairs. A tall man with his hands in his jacket pockets descended the steps. Stopping midway on the steps, he asked, "Everything okay?"

"Yes." Bev frowned at him. She tilted her head and nodded toward the upstairs. "Let me finish here, and we'll talk outside. You didn't need to come here."

"We should probably look at the other properties. Mikko's expecting an update before dinner," Delanie said.

The man looked down at both women and descended several more steps. "I think you're done looking today. Bev, we need to talk now."

"Dan," Bev snarled through gritted teeth. "I'm busy. I need to finish here with Elise, and then we'll talk."

He stomped down several more steps. "We need to talk now. You keep saying it's over, but it's not if people keep asking questions. And why do you keep texting me if it wasn't an issue? You said this place was basically abandoned."

"Bev, if there's a problem, I can call another realtor." Delanie was pleased that her investigation had made them uncomfortable.

The realtor scowled at Dan, and then her look softened. "No, we can work this out."

"Shut up. Bev, you said this would be the perfect house for what we needed. You wanted her out of the picture. I should have never listened to you."

"Dan, don't say another word," Bev snarled, nostrils flaring. Delanie backed toward the door.

"Don't move," Dan commanded.

"Dan!" Bev yelled. "Don't be stupid. Shut up and wait for me outside. You're ruining everything."

Dan's glance darted around the room. He had the look of a cornered animal.

The floor upstairs creaked.

Delanie heard the sound again.

A shriek broke the silence and echoed through the empty basement. Stephen Charles, the listing agent, hurtled down the stairs toward Dan. He landed on the taller man's back, and they tumbled down the last few steps.

While they were scrapping, Delanie pulled out her phone.

"I knew it was you," Stephen yelled, pointing to Bev.

"I don't know what you're talking about," the other realtor sneered.

"Bev, don't be coy. You're in this up to your pretty lil neck," Dan said.

"Enough! Stay where you are and keep your hands where I can see them." Delanie punched 9-1-1 on her phone.

Delanie relaxed slightly. She was glad her investigation could bring closure for Kristi and her family. She took pride in that she was persistent enough to look where the police didn't. Now it was time for them to sort this out.

And it was definitely time for another girls' night out with more pink punch.

BRAYKING GLASS
by Eleanor Cawood Jones

Martha McBain was in an obvious foul mood. The highly suspicious death of Mr. Glazier was threatening to shut down the fourth and final day of the renowned Cavalier Wine Festival in Plains, Virginia, and she was clearly having none of it.

"I've had these tickets for months! *Months!*" she practically shouted into the phone at her BFF and fellow wine enthusiast, Lorrie George. "We were going to find a new wine for my thirty-fifth birthday bash, I was going to do all my Christmas shopping (any friend or relative of Martha's knew what they were getting for any gift-giving occasion, even if they didn't know the exact vintage), and I was even going to find a few suggestions for Father Martin to try to break up the monotony of the same old, same old for communion!"

"Slow down, Marth," Lorrie said. "Who is Mr. Glazier, what's wrong at the festival, and why are you shouting? Aren't we still on for the festival tomorrow after church? We've never missed a year since it started. And do you really think Father Martin is worried about his monotonous wine more than your immortal soul?"

"You know Mr. Glazier, Lorrie. He owns the glass shop in downtown Leesburg on Main Street. He won that award last year for inventing a new color for those blown-glass hummingbirds he has in his store."

"Oh yeah. That guy. I know the glass shop. They replaced my sliding porch door for me last year. But I didn't know the glass shop was owned by a Mr. Glazier. That's crazy! Who owns the pottery shop next door, Mr. Potter? Ha ha! And did I ever tell you my dermatologist back where I grew up in Kentucky was named Dr. Rash? That time I had the mole he told me he felt his career choice was inevitable, and—"

"Lorrie! Focus! Did you not hear what I read you from the paper? Mr. Glazier is dead. He died at the wine festival. Here, I'll read you this online article from *Virginia Right Now*:

Area merchants joined local residents this evening for an impromptu get-together at Sharper Edge Glass Shop in charming downtown Leesburg, Virginia, to celebrate the life of Franklin Glazier, preeminent glass blower and skilled artisan. Mr. Glazier's life was cut short earlier today when local Cavalier Wine Festival attendees found his body in the pasture alongside the merchant tents dotting the fields of Plains, Virginia.

"We had no idea he was, you know, dead," said Emily Frisch, Plains resident and local bartender, who found the deceased. "Everybody and their brother goes and has a nap in that field after a day of tasting the local wines. We figured he was just sleeping it off, you know? Even though it was kind of early in the morning. Then the security guy tried to wake him up and Mr. Glazier was having none of it, I mean, seeing how he was dead and all. They told us he had a big gash on the back of his head and, after they moved him, you could see bits of broken glass all around, like somebody had bashed him with a vase or a heavy glass or something."

Mr. King and his assistant Vinny at the festival's King Family Petting Zoo added that they couldn't believe Mr. Glazier was gone, as they'd just seen him the day before feeding some popcorn and a sno-cone to a baby goat. "What a pity," Vinny said. "Anyone that would share his raspberry sno-cone with a little animal like that must have had a good heart." (Mr. King cautions all petting zoo visitors, however, to stick with the official petting-zoo food when feeding the animals.)

Mr. Glazier was 65 years of age and a longtime Leesburg resident.

Additional details to follow as they become available.

"Eeeeew! Death by glass!" Lorrie made a choking noise. "Do you think there was a lot of blood?"

"And wait, Lorrie. That's not all. Fred—you know Freddy Bob Gronbeck. We went to elementary school with all five of the

Gronbecks. Fred is the oldest. You remember. Did you know he's stone cold bald now? He's the head security guard for the festival. I called him up and you know what he told me? He said Mr. Glazier had been there *all night*! His girlfriend said he never came home. He was seen late yesterday evening at the festival, talking with Marge from Marge's Mixes, the sno-cone booth. You know how the wine festival is all family friendly and all. The sno-cone booth is over at the entrance, by the Ferris wheel and the petting zoo. They added it this year."

"Oooh, I wonder if they have blueberry. I love a good blueberry sno-cone."

"They probably do. We'll stop there first if they open the festival back up. Fred doesn't know if Marge is officially a suspect. He likes raspberry sno-cones."

They took a moment to decide together that blueberry was best, raspberry second, and orange a close third. Neither of them had much use for lime.

"But, anyway, Lorrie, Fred says Marge may be a suspect because back in the day, before Mr. Glazier started winning his awards, Marge was his girlfriend and I heard she wasn't too supportive of his art because—Hello! Starving artist!—and finally Mr. Glazier went off and left her for his current girlfriend, Georgina. Georgina was more than willing to put in extra hours at the hair salon to support him before he hit it big with the shop, because she always says when she perms me that Mr. Glazier is good as gold and sooooo talented. Of course, he pays all her bills now. Did you know he put in custom mirrors in Georgina's salon since the last time we got the pedicures, you remember, for our Welcome to Spring pick-me-up party at work? Wow, they are gorgeous mirrors. Etched glass with little scissors and combs and what-not right on them. Really classes up the joint. Big mirrors and little handheld ones, too."

Lorrie let on to Martha she needed to see those mirrors, and added that another girls-day-out pedicure wouldn't go amiss. She took a look in her own looking glass and tried to decide if her golden split ends warranted an appointment soon. She wondered if she could ever have hair like Georgina, big and blond and teased tall. It was striking, and the gentlemen liked it. She'd have to remember to ask.

Martha went on. "And Georgina was also there last night. Fred says there's some speculating already that Georgina went over to the festival for the sole purpose of spying on Mr. Glazier, as he'd been out way later than he said and maybe somebody told her he was talking to Marge and sampling a cone with her. And then Fred tells me maybe Marge didn't take kindly to Georgina showing up and maybe she and Mr. Glazier got into it about the past and when he dumped her and all." She paused. "I hear Mr. Glazier has had second thoughts about leaving Marge and that he thinks Georgina may be a gold digger."

"Really? So maybe Georgina got wind of that, took one of those fancy custom mirrors over to the festival, and cut to the chase with Mr. Glazier," Lorrie said. "Bam! Right over the head in a temporary fit of sno-cone-induced insanity. Of course, that's pure speculation. But maybe it's not Georgina. I suppose Marge could have had some glass dishes at the cone stand, or what not; that also would have done the job."

"And don't forget all those expensive, engraved wine glasses at hand. Anyone could have bashed Mr. Glazier with one of the heavy commemorative ones if they snuck it out of the admissions booth. Anyone at all."

There was a moment of silence while they contemplated who anyone at all might be.

"That festival is a heck of a bargain, though, Martha. Just think—for only twenty-five dollars, including a delicate, beautifully engraved, collectible wine glass, you get to go from tent to tent, getting a small sample from each vintner poured into your glass, and making your purchase decisions. No limit on samples."

"Yeah," Martha agreed. "And the more you taste, the more you buy. What a gimmick!"

Lorrie was fine with that. She liked supporting the local

merchants. And she liked wine. Plus, if you wanted a real keeper souvenir, you could plunk down a steep extra fifty dollars at admission and get a heftier glass, which would be great on the mantel or in a curio cabinet, or on top of your wine fridge, come to think of it. Maybe this year she'd pay the extra fifty bucks.

"Martha, maybe Mr. Glazier just slipped and hit his head in the field, fell on somebody's glass or something."

They thought about this for half a minute.

"Not nearly as interesting," Martha finally decided. "My bet's on Marge or Georgina."

Lorrie pulled up the *Virginia Right Now* article on her laptop. "There's an update on that article you read me, Martha. It says the show must go on, that the police have cordoned off the area in the field where Mr. Glazier went to the great glass-blowing furnace in the sky, and they thoroughly searched the grounds, even the Ferris wheel and the petting zoo area, and that we can all commence to drinking tomorrow afternoon on the last day of the festival. That's not an exact quote, by the way."

"No? Well, it ought to be." Martha was openly proud of Lorrie for her poetic way of speaking, and for her written prose, which was regularly featured in the company newsletter. "But Fred told me something else."

"There's more? More suspects than Marge and Georgina? Wow, this glass guy got around."

"It's not like that." Martha dropped her voice to a whisper. "There's foul play afoot at the festival, Watson."

Lorrie whisper-giggled. "Do tell."

"Fred says it's hush-hush, so keep it under wraps."

"Pinky swear." Lorrie mentally hooked pinkies with Martha on the other side of town.

"There's a bunch of missing items at the festival this year. Rings, watches, wallets, jewelry. All small things, but a lot more action with people looking for things at the lost-and-found tent, filing police reports, complaining to the admissions staff. Fred said they were even going to put in some security cameras to see if they couldn't catch whoever it is, and it's too bad they didn't have them up before Mr. Glazier got it in the head. No one has been caught stealing at all, but it seems there's at least a pickpocket or two on site this year, taking advantage of all the tipsy tourists."

"The Tipsy Tourist would be a great name for a beach bar, wouldn't it?" Lorrie could just picture it. Cute little beach tables, sand on the floor, drinks served in mini beach buckets, and maybe some cute souvenir glasses made by whoever was going to run Mr. Glazier's shop now.

"Hey, Martha, who is inheriting Mr. Glazier's shop now? Does he have kids or grandkids? Or do you think maybe Marge or Georgina will inherit? They say follow the money, you know."

"Well, hey there, Nancy Drew. I was thinking that maybe Mr. Glazier ran into the pickpocket and threatened to turn him in, but sure, some greedy relative certainly could have taken advantage of his slightly inebriated state—one assumes he was drinking; it *is* a wine festival—to clunk him over the head with some spare glass from the shop, sure."

"Watson."

"Excuse me?"

"Watson. Not Nancy Drew. I liked it better when you called me Watson. I can be Watson to your Sherlock."

"Oh, gotcha. Well, Watson. I'll see what I can find out from my Leesburg connections about whether Mr. Glazier has kids or who gets the shop, but just so's you know, Fred is leaning heavily toward the petty pickpocket thief being the culprit. There's a lot of big money that goes to the festival, and apparently most of the items missing are on the pricey side. And one more thing, and you have to double pinky swear on this one."

Lorrie commenced to do so.

Martha's voice dropped to a whisper. "Fred says Mr. Glazier's pride and joy, his Presidential Rolex with the pearl face and diamond bezel, was missing when they found him. Fred thinks Mr.

Glazier would have fought for that watch. It's worth *thousands*. And you can't tell anyone at all, not even Father Martin, because the cops aren't releasing that bit of information, and Fred could get fired if they find out he told. He likes his job as head of security at these kinds of events. He says it's been a lucrative career and he's always meeting interesting people."

She paused. "Also, he's not really bald, you know. He shaves his head. Gives him that tough-guy security image and all."

"Martha?"

"Mmmm?"

"Martha, when you were talking to Fred, did you make a date with him by any chance?"

"No girl wants to spend her thirty-fifth birthday alone, Watson."

Lorrie smiled to herself. Martha hadn't been on a date since her divorce two years earlier. If she wanted to go out with Mr. Clean security guard, that was fine with her. Fred had been kind of cute in elementary school, come to think of it. Of course, he'd had hair then. "Pick you up tomorrow right after church, Sherlock. Don't forget the tickets."

Lorrie made up her mind then and there to buy two heavy souvenir glasses at this year's festival, one for herself and one for her BFF Martha, as part of Martha's landmark birthday gift.

And if Lorrie noticed Martha was heavily made up and perfumed the next morning at church, she didn't say a thing as the two of them set off for the fields of Plains after the service.

The line of cars exiting the highway to get to the festival was extra long this year, and they speculated that the murder had created some heightened interest. They passed the time revisiting their theories over who had done in Mr. Glazier. Martha had discovered from her cousin Lou-Lou in Leesburg that Mr. Glazier had never been married and had no children. Lou-Lou didn't know who Mr. Glazier's heir was and told Martha she wondered if he'd left everything to charity, as he had a real soft spot for animal rescue and the local policemen's benevolent fund. And the *Virginia Right*

Now site had no new information to speak of.

After the long drive they wasted no time checking in, getting their festival map so they could find their way around, and picking up their delicate souvenir wine-tasting glasses.

Martha's aunt Betty Buckles was running the admissions stand, and Lorrie pulled her aside so Betty could save her a few of the heavy glasses to purchase later in the day.

To Lorrie's amusement, Martha was openly disappointed not to see Fred right away, but they soon forgot everything except rushing to their favorite tents to sample this year's blends. A few hours later, Martha had ordered two cases of wine for home delivery, and stuffed four select bottles in her backpack. Lorrie liked a sweet drink and had filled her backpack with Virginia's Best Cider, which she did every year. By then, they were sunburned, tired, and happy, and more than eager to head over to the refreshment tent. They were a little tipsy, but more relaxed than anything. Martha always said you should buy wine with a clear head. Lorrie was actually a little past tipsy, truth be told, but Martha always drove home, so that was fine.

Lorrie's favorite festival stop was secretly always the King Family Petting Zoo, and she couldn't wait to head there after they'd shared a couple of burgers at the refreshment tent. She greeted Mr. King and his wife, laughed at the baby ducks, ogled the llama, admired the peacock, and cooed over the baby goats. She even fed the littlest one from a bottle while Martha held her backpack and looked around for Fred. They finished petting the animals and turned to head toward the Ferris wheel for their annual ride.

"Oomph!" Lorrie felt something nudge her from behind, and turned to find the smallest burro she'd ever seen head-butting her. She burst out laughing.

Mr. King saw the little animal's antics and came running. "No, little B! No! Don't bump the customers! Sorry, girls. Seems this little guy likes the smell of grapes. Makes him a bit antsy."

Lorrie dropped to her knees. "Oh, aren't you cute! What's your name, little fella?" She ran her hand through his wiry coat and he leaned closer.

"We just call him Bray," said Mr. King. "My new helper Vinny named him, says he brays real good for his size and that his full name is Bray King." He laughed. "I got me a stable hand with a sense of humor." He gestured toward a good-looking cowboy type over by the baby ducks. "Vinny's a real keeper." He waggled his eyebrows at Lorrie. "Single, too. New in town. Probably kinda lonely."

Bray the burro stuck his nose in Lorrie's wine glass before she could reply, and she got the giggles. Mr. King turned away and Bray's surprisingly large pink tongue started to lick the inside of the wine glass. There was a little liquid left in the bottom and she didn't think it would hurt him. He was so cute, so funny. She wondered if she could find a free hand to get out her cell phone and take a picture of the thirsty little guy.

Crunch!

"Bray, no!" Apparently Bray had lapped up all the wine and was making an attempt to eat the glass. Lorrie snatched it away. Thank goodness it was only cracked all around the rim, and not broken. She couldn't bear the thought of possibly hurting the little beast if he'd taken a chunk out of the glass and eaten it. But the souvenir glass was well and truly ruined. She was bummed at being out twenty-five bucks, but it would make a good story.

Startled, and missing his wine glass, Bray reacted. He gave a great "eee-awww" and head-butted her again. Taken by surprise, she fell backward over a small fence and into a big pile of loose hay behind the goat pen. She sat still for a moment. She heard Martha laughing, and stared up at her and a gorgeous bald guy in a security uniform.

"I see you found Fred," she managed to say. Fred reached to pull her up, grinning away, but the handsome cowboy came running. He practically elbowed Fred out of the way and bent down, looking closely at her and all around her.

"You okay? You hurt? You trip over something or what?" Oh, good. Handsome cowboy type hadn't seen her get burro-butted. Of course, he probably thought she was a complete klutz.

"Nothing broken, fortunately, cowboy." Wow, she really was tipsy. Martha snickered and Fred grinned wider, then his smile faded.

"Hey, Lorrie, what happened to your ankle? You're bleeding. Mr. King, go grab that first-aid kit from the admissions booth."

Vinny the stranger cowboy nudged Fred out of the way again. "Just a scratch." He reached out with a strong grip and got Lorrie to her feet. He pushed his way between her and the hay.

Wow, those brown eyes were killer. And just the right height for slow dancing. And—yep, she was definitely more than tipsy. She opened her mouth to ask if he really was single when Bray let loose with another ear-splitting screech.

She mentally crossed "burro" off her house pets list. And added "cowboy." Oh dear. Was that sexist?

Now Fred was shoving Vinny out of the way. "That's a pretty good scratch. Let's see what it is you ran up against in that hay. You might need a tetanus shot."

"Dr. Rash could set you up with that." Martha and Lorrie looked at each other and giggled. Maybe Martha had passed tipsy, too.

Fred leaned over and began carefully going through the hay, when suddenly he face-planted in it as Vinny gave him a shove. The cowboy then turned tail and ran out of the petting zoo area, jumping over two startled baby goats along the way.

Fred rolled over and came up holding a shiny wristwatch and a sparkly necklace. "Catch that guy!" he hollered through a mouthful of hay, and darned if Mr. King, older now but once a star tight end at Virginia Tech, caught up to Vinny and tackled him, hard, right before he got to the parking lot.

So, the wine festival had its pickpocket, caught not by Sherlock, Watson, or even Nancy Drew, had she happened along. Nope, the crime-solving detective turned out to be a sweet, wine-loving, glass-breaking little burro who went by the name of Bray.

There were a lot of valuable objects hidden in that hay. Vinny would have easily been able to get them out of the festival when he cleaned up the area and loaded the hay and animals into the petting zoo truck that night.

And as events unfolded, it would turn out to be Vinny who had attacked Mr. Glazier with one of the heavy wine glasses. The police were able to piece that much together. They theorized Mr. Glazier had caught Vinny taking his watch and, as Martha, Lorrie, and eventually *Virginia Right Now* speculated, he had fought back. But no one would ever know the details for sure. That was one cowboy who wasn't talking.

And I—as you've probably already surmised, it's me, Lorrie, who's been writing this tale—was out my dream date, and Mr. King was out one stable hand, but Mr. Glazier was out so much more. It was so sad he lost his life over his prized possession, which was just a material object, after all.

But something good did come out of it. It turned out Mr. Glazier did leave the glass shop to Marge. In his will, he called her the love of his life, and last we heard she was thinking about trading in sno-cones for glassblowing, at least during the winter months. She plans to keep the glass shop going, and he's left her quite well off. I'm sure she's wistful, though, wondering if they would have gotten back together eventually.

It's bittersweet, a bit like my own situation. I mean, sure, this year's collectible wine glass was completely ruined by a toothy burro with a strong desire to drink, but did I mention Fred has four brothers, all of whom grew up as handsome as Fred? The middle one is single, and Saturday night Martha and I have a double date planned.

She's bringing the wine. I'm bringing a sore arm from a tetanus shot I needed since I cut my ankle on a diamond-encrusted Rolex hidden in a pile of hay.

We all have to work with what we've got, after all.

Cheers!

HOW DO YOU MEND A BROKEN HEART?
by Maggie King

"You *really* think we'll find ourselves a couple of rich husbands tonight?"

I laughed. "Just yesterday, you quoted from that book you love so much…something about rich men on the hunt for wives."

My sister Kate fussed with the neckline of her black lace top and recited from memory: "'It is a truth universally acknowledged, that a single man in possession of a good fortune, must be in want of a wife.'"

"That's the one."

"It's from *Pride and Prejudice* by Jane Austen."

"You always were the bookworm of the family."

Moments before, Kate and I had arrived at the very fancy Mavis I. Paxton House, home of the River Edge Club, a private social club for Richmond, Virginia's elite. After spending a mint on tickets for the *Springtime Is Sweet* fundraiser, we wanted to look our best, and ducked into an elegant ladies' lounge for a primping session before making a grand entrance in the ballroom. Plus, we had those prospective rich husbands to consider.

The pricey tickets benefitted The Pantry, a Richmond food bank whose mission was to feed those in need—a mission near and dear to our Aunt Pauline's heart. Aunt Pauline was dying of pancreatic cancer and couldn't attend the fundraiser, so she had asked Kate and me to drive down from Northern Virginia to support her favorite cause. We never could say no to our beloved aunt.

Kate said, "If we're playing Jane Austen characters, I get to be Elizabeth Bennett, with first dibs on Mr. Darcy."

"Who?"

Kate huffed her frustration. "They're the main characters in *Pride and Prejudice.*"

Kate spent her high school years holed up in her room, studying and reading the likes of Jane Austen. I ran with a wild crowd and was lucky to graduate. Eventually I found my talent in computers, but still rarely opened a book.

"Aunt Pauline said we'd have our pick of rich guys tonight," I said.

"Actually, Becca, she said *I* might find a rich husband and that tarty outfit you have on makes you mistress material." Kate finished touching up her makeup, plopped down in a red velvet love seat, and leaned her head back against the fancy gold paper that covered the walls.

I smiled as I refreshed my Red Sin lipstick. Aunt Pauline always spoke her mind. I glanced at Kate. She sat with crossed legs, the slit of her slinky skirt revealing a daring expanse of thigh. "What about you with that slit up to your unmentionables? That's assuming you're even wearing unmentionables."

"We won't mention them," Kate quipped. She fanned the fingers of her right hand, surveying her French manicure.

"I think I'm pretty modest tonight," I said. "Just a hint of cleavage." Although I'd probably gone overboard on raising the hemline of my white satin form-fitting dress. I'd worn the same dress when I married Arnie. Arnie, my now ex, a champ in the bedroom and at the shooting range—useless anyplace else.

"Did you see that great-looking guy when we arrived?" Kate asked. "The one standing behind the registration table?"

"Yes! Gorgeous Man!" I held a hand over my heart, miming a swoon. "Wasn't he to die for? Maybe he's rich."

"Let's snag a dance with him."

"Becca, do you ever wonder if that terrible business with Mama and Daddy caused Aunt Pauline's cancer? I've heard that anger and resentment can do that. And she has a heap of resentment toward that man who lent Daddy that money."

I fluffed my blond mane. "Let's hope she's an exception."

When our mama was diagnosed with a rare lung disease, Daddy tried his best to take care of her. But the medications were expensive and not covered by insurance. Daddy worked as an accountant for a large property management firm, and his salary only went so far in helping Mama. Her own job as a housekeeper didn't help much and didn't last long after her diagnosis. When Mama died, Daddy lost his will to live without her and took an overdose of barbiturates.

Our parents shielded Kate and me from their money woes and gave us the bare minimum of information. Aunt Pauline filled in the grim details of how her hapless brother and sister-in-law took out a loan—a loan that sounded like a godsend at the time but turned out to be anything but.

"I'd known this man for many years from church and thought him the nicest guy in the world," Aunt Pauline had said. "When I told him about Marcella's illness and how Davey wanted to get the expensive medication she needed, this man was quick to offer to loan them the money. When Davey had trouble paying back the loan, this nice man turned into a Jekyll and Hyde and pressured him to embezzle from his company. I'm sure that's what drove my little brother to his death."

Tears spilled down Aunt Pauline's face. Voice dripping with sarcasm, she added, "The bastard graciously forgave the loan and didn't go after me or you girls. Then he went overseas somewhere, became a missionary, of all things. Last I heard he died in a car accident in some African country. Good riddance."

Kate and I made decent money—she as a Professor of English Literature at a Northern Virginia college, and me as I.T. director for a Washington-area software firm—and we paid Daddy's employer the full amount Daddy had embezzled. I wish we'd known how desperate Daddy had been, but his pride wouldn't have let him accept our help.

"Kate, let's forget all about illness and heartbreak and have a good time tonight. We deserve a little fun. Maybe we *will* find ourselves rich husbands. Or, in my case, a rich lover." I leaned against the marble counter and continued to assess my image in the huge mirror with the gold antique frame. Bouquets of yellow roses filled the room with sweet fragrance. The sconces flanking the

155

mirror gave off flattering light that made the rhinestone pendants swinging from my ears sparkle. "If we found rich husbands, we could be wearing real bling and not fakes."

"You're right about that," Kate drawled. "When did they start calling flashy jewelry *bling*?"

"Dunno."

Kate stood. "Are you ever going to finish primping? This thing will be over, and you'll still be here, admiring yourself."

"Okay, *okay*." After a final fluff of the hair and a quick check for lipstick on my teeth, I picked up my program and looped my too-big rhinestone-studded satin bag over my shoulder. The event called for an elegant evening clutch, but I carried too many items.

"I'm ready."

Kate preferred an understated style and kept her jewelry to a minimum. Discreet earrings and a cubic zirconia choker completed her accessorizing. She bore an uncanny resemblance to former Alaska Governor and vice-presidential candidate Sarah Palin, a look she capitalized on with designer glasses and tousled auburn curls.

"Daddy would have had a blast at this place," Kate said as we walked out of the lounge. "He just loved to dance, didn't he?"

"He sure did." My voice caught. Even after three years, I still choked up thinking of Daddy.

Kate and I walked along a hallway, stopping at the various rooms to ooh and aah at the ornate marble fireplaces, crystal chandeliers, and Persian rugs.

"Where's Gorgeous Man?" I asked as we passed the registration table.

"I'm sure he's around somewhere. He's hard to miss." Kate pulled on my arm. "Let's check out the silent auction."

We continued walking. Healthy-looking ficus plants lined another hallway leading to an immense ballroom. An amped-up band set up on the raised stage played hits from my parents' era. Red-flocked wallpaper covered the walls. My ex would have loudly proclaimed, "Man oh man, we're in a bordello!"

Richmonders had turned out in droves to do their part in combatting the local hunger problem. Every style of dress met my eyes: jeans with button-down shirts, tailored suits, floor-length formals. Glittering gems dripped from the women. People sat at round tables, danced, or milled around, laughing and yelling at each other to be heard above the din of the band.

My abbreviated dress got the admiring looks I'd expected. But I remained focused on Gorgeous Man, specifically on his whereabouts.

"Where *is* he?" I looked around, but the only men I saw sported potbellies.

The silent auction tables took up one wall of the ballroom. Offerings included vacation stays, golf outings, wine baskets, gift certificates for online retailers, babysitting and landscaping services, to name a few.

I bid on a spa day and a basket of what was surely a lifetime's supply of tea paraphernalia. A group of women tried to outbid each other on a three-week South American cruise. After bidding on a few more items, Kate and I left the auction area before getting carried away.

The *Springtime Is Sweet* fundraiser was aptly named, as it featured a dessert buffet in April. Kate and I scanned tables laden with a mouth-watering selection of sweet treats—cookies, fruit tartlets, éclairs, mini pancake stacks, parfaits, and more—provided by trendy Richmond restaurants and caterers. Everything was springtime pink, from the tablecloths to the huge bouquets that formed a backdrop to the array of desserts. Dogwood branches canopied a huge platter of grapes and strawberries.

We walked through a door that opened to a garden. Tables holding more desserts beckoned, but the acrid smell of tobacco smoke from high-spirited donors drove us back inside.

Kate and I filled plates with a variety of bite-sized items and found two seats together at one of the tables. With the floor-length tablecloth—pink of course—I felt free to slip off my strappy sandals and give my feet a rest from my five-inch heels. My friends wore the things with great poise and balance. Apparently, I didn't have the gene.

"It's kind of ironic to have all this upscale food at a do to raise money for a food bank," I said as I enjoyed some especially creamy cheesecake.

Kate laughed. "I hardly think the organization would attract all these people, many with money up the wazoo, if they served Twinkies." She popped a lemon square in her mouth.

The band took a break and a man wearing a tailored blue suit appeared on the dance floor.

I grabbed Kate's arm. "There's Gorgeous Man!"

"Hello, everyone, I'm Jeremy Redman, CEO of The Pantry. Welcome to the *Springtime Is Sweet* fundraiser!" The crowd cheered. Jeremy went on to thank everyone for their generosity and reminded them of the silent auction and other opportunities to demonstrate even greater generosity.

He finished his spiel and started a short video promoting the good work of The Pantry. A couple of lively games followed. When the band started up again and the dance floor filled with twisting bodies energized by sugar highs, my eyes tracked Jeremy as he moved to the silent auction area.

Kate nudged me. "Now's your chance. Go grab him. I'll watch your bag."

"How do I look?"

"Fantastic, for a tart," Kate said with a wink. "Just freshen up your lipstick."

After taking care of that task and finding my sandals under the table, I got up and approached Gorgeous Man.

"Hi, I'm Becca Highsmith." I added a flutter of eyelashes.

"Jeremy Redman." Bass voice, very seductive. His dark hair gleamed. He took my hand and kissed it, his lips soft and warm.

"This is a *fabulous* event." I spread my arms as if to encompass the crowd.

He smiled and his eyes swept me, head to foot, lingering on my hint of cleavage.

When a slow dance started, Jeremy leaned close and, voice husky, asked, "Care to dance?"

I let a smile signal my agreement. Jeremy put his hand on my back as we made our way to the crowded dance floor. When he took me in his arms, I felt the fabric of his suit, soft against the firmness of his muscles. I closed my eyes and wished the dance would never end.

But it did end and we slowly parted. With any luck, the lighting was dim enough that Jeremy couldn't see my face flushing. When the band upped the tempo, we stayed on the floor for a faster dance.

I focused on staying upright on my sky-high heels, relieved that I didn't take a spill. I tossed my blond curls in what I hoped was a provocative way, not one that made me look like I suffered from a fit. My earrings slapped the side of my face as they swayed and jingled. After three more dances, we laughingly decided to take a break.

"Can I get you something to drink?" Jeremy flashed a smile worthy of a toothpaste ad. His blue eyes sparkled brighter than any gem in the place.

"I'd love some white wine."

While Jeremy went to the bar, I returned to the table where I'd left my bag. Kate talked to a man wearing a Stetson. Even over the earsplitting band, I heard the man's loud guffaw as he called Kate "Governor." Apparently my sister was playing up her resemblance to Sarah Palin.

By the time Jeremy returned with two glasses of wine, I'd crossed my tanned legs, letting the skirt of my satin dress slide up my thigh alarmingly. I introduced him to Kate, and she in turn introduced the Stetson-wearing man, whose name I didn't catch over the music.

Jeremy sat close to me—very close. I grabbed a program from the table and fanned myself. I'd never had such a response to a man

I'd met minutes before, not even my ex. I wasn't one for hookups on short acquaintance. But I could be persuaded. Just this once.

"Stop it, Becca!" I ordered myself. What would Mama say if she could see me now, acting like a wanton hussy?

Jeremy and I sipped our wine and gazed into each other's eyes. He leaned close and whispered into my curls, "Becca, you're absolutely gorgeous!"

"You're pretty handsome yourself." I hadn't meant to sound like a husky-voiced woman from one of those old movies Mama and Daddy used to watch, but I suspected that I did.

"Can I offer you a tour of this place? It's a beautiful building."

"Ooh, I'd *love* a tour." I bet he had more in mind than a tour...and that suited me just fine.

I tapped Kate on the shoulder. "I'm going on a tour." I added a wink.

She winked back. "You two behave yourselves, now!"

*

Jeremy led me out of the ballroom, along the ficus-lined hallway, past the same ornate rooms that had attracted Kate and me earlier, and up a magnificent staircase to the second floor of the house. With one hand tucked in Jeremy's arm and the other clutching my wine glass, I felt "on top of the world," one of Daddy's favorite expressions. I didn't tell Jeremy that my mama had worked as housekeeper at the Mavis I. Paxton House for many years and that I knew the place inside and out. Let him play tour guide. I made murmurs of appreciation as we walked.

Most of the second floor functioned as office space for the River Edge Club. My favorite room was the library, a large space with floor-to-ceiling shelves of books on gardening and Richmond history.

"Oh, is that a library? I just *adore* libraries."

Jeremy and I walked around the room, admiring the crystal chandelier that hung over a large table. Tall windows looked out on historic buildings. I kept up my *golly-gee* demeanor. Jeremy smiled.

Another hallway ended at a door that took us to yet another set of stairs. We ascended to the third floor and slipped into a large meeting room. Moonlight streamed through the windows, revealing rows of cushioned chairs facing a podium and pulldown projector screen. Framed floral prints covered the walls. I threw my bag on one of the chairs and set my wine glass on the floor.

Jeremy pulled me close. His kiss was gentle at first, then hard and searing. He ran his hands down my back, pressing his body against mine. My fingers raked his hair, silky as a Persian cat's. We stayed like that for a few moments until I pulled away, panting.

"Inhaler." I patted my chest. "Asthma."

"Are you all right, Becca?"

"I will be," I managed as I staggered to the chair where I'd dumped my bag. "You just got me," *gasp*, "so excited," *gasp*."

No doubt Jeremy cursed his luck in winding up with an asthmatic and was planning his escape.

His next words confirmed my suspicion. "You know, Becca, I should probably get back downstairs—"

I opened my bag and reached inside for the item I needed. Spinning around, I said, "I don't think so, Jeremy."

The first bullet went through Jeremy Redman's chest. Right between the nipples. To be safe, I added another.

Thank you, Arnie, for all those times you dragged me to the shooting range. You weren't so useless after all.

I tossed the rest of my wine on Jeremy, now sprawled on the floor, and dropped the empty glass in my bag, along with the Smith and Wesson M&P, blond wig, and torturous sandals. I hightailed it out of there.

*

Aunt Pauline died two weeks later, happy to see justice done for the death of her brother and sister-in-law.

"I hope Jeremy Redman burns in hell," she said when Kate and I visited her in hospice.

When Aunt Pauline had learned that Jeremy Redman was alive and well, not having died during his stint as a missionary, and now CEO of The Pantry, she decided she wouldn't leave this world with "that bastard" still in it. She regretted being too sick to manage the deed herself, but found her nieces willing and able to be her surrogates. How could we deny our beloved aunt her dying wish? I only wish the guy hadn't been so *hot*.

After fleeing the Mavis I. Paxton House, Kate and I drove around downtown Richmond, stopping at dumpsters along the way to deposit our outfits, shoes, Kate's glasses, and Aunt Pauline's wigs. I wanted to keep the satin dress for sentimental reasons but figured that with the gunshot residue it had to go. Besides, it had done its job and done it well. Regretfully, I added it to the pile of refuse in the last dumpster.

Aunt Pauline's gun, wiped clean of prints, ended up in the James River.

Will the police ever catch up with us? Incidentally, Becca and Kate aren't our real names. In my dreams I could hear the click of handcuffs as the cold metal squeezed my wrists. Could we get O.J. Simpson's Dream Team of lawyers to defend us? That would take cash, and plenty of it.

The hunt for rich husbands goes on.

HERE'S TO YOU, MRS. ROBINSON
by Teresa Inge

"Thanks for shopping with us." Margot Berry placed items in a bag and handed it to the last customer of the day. Just as she turned off the Open sign, the doorbell jangled, and Tessa Robinson rushed through the door flustered and breathless. "Oh, gawd. Please help me, Margot!"

"Tessa...how can I help?"

"I need a few last-minute items." Tessa, the great granddaughter of a wealthy plastics manufacturer, and Margot's frenemy since high school insisted.

"For tonight's party?" Margot referred to Tessa's annual wine tasting, one designed for guests to taste Tessa's favorite organic wines and guests score their preferences on a card. But this year Margot planned a real surprise. "What do you need?"

"Do you have any of the cocktail charms with the pink beads and metal hooks left?"

"Yes." Margot walked toward the wine accessories table. "How many would you like?"

"How many do you have?"

Margot counted the charms. "Three."

"I'll take them."

After Tessa picked up additional supplies, Margot rang up the items at the register.

"I presume you're still coming tonight?"

"Of course. I wouldn't miss it for the world."

"You know," Tessa said, "I'm glad you and I made up after that little business with Harry and me last year."

Margot swallowed a growl after hearing Harry's name on Tessa's cheating lips. She was referring to her affair with Margot's then-husband "Harry." "Yes. I'm glad too." She lied.

"Great. Oh...and speaking of Harry. He'll be there tonight since

163

we're back together."

"Yes, I heard."

After saying goodbye to Tessa, Margot locked the door of The Beach Shop in Nags Head, North Carolina. She had opened the business after leaving her graphic design job and cheating husband. The small cottage was a tourist stop for those visiting the Outer Banks—the OBX—a spit of land between the Atlantic Ocean and the Pamlico Sound, and a mecca for beach vacationers.

Margot grabbed her purse and headed home. This would be her fifth year attending Tessa's party. Since high school, she and Tessa had been involved in a love-hate relationship. Lately, it was more hate on Margot's part, since Tessa, in a drunken state, announced her affair with Harry at last year's wine tasting. Tonight would be payback.

After dressing in a light blue sundress and sandals, Margot slipped a bottle of wine into a large handbag and drove to Tessa's house on the south end in Nags Head, a few minutes away. The magnificent beachfront property had belonged to the Robinson family since 1965. Tessa had inherited the estate and hired Margot's husband Harry, a wealthy builder, to renovate it a couple of years ago. Before the affair.

Tessa's butler Edwin met Margot at the door. "Good evening. Mrs. Robinson and her guests are on the back patio. Hors d'oeuvres and cocktails are being served outside." He gestured toward the back deck.

Margot stepped onto the patio taking in the stunning beach view as she walked to the bar.

She viewed the drink specials written on a chalk board. "Interesting. A pink lemonade vodka drink with simple syrup, lemon juice, and sparkling water. That sounds perfect for a June evening. I'll have the Robinson special."

"Good choice. It's Mrs. Robinson's favorite cocktail, and of course she loves pink."

"Yes, I know," Margot said.

"And what will you have, sir?"

"The same. Except light on the lemonade." Harry spoke up from behind Margot. Margot turned and faced her ex. "So, you and Tessa are back together?"

"Yeah...we made up." Harry took his beverage with the charm on the glass rim from the bartender. It was the charm Tessa had purchased earlier.

"Thought you were a scotch man," Margot said.

Harry laughed. "Tessa must be growing on me."

Harry was up to something, since he loathed Tessa for exposing their affair.

"Look. I'm sorry for what happened. Are you ever going to forgive me?" Harry said.

Margot mulled over how the affair had broken up their marriage. She did want to move forward with Harry. "I don't know."

"Maybe one day we can share a drink, like old times."

"Maybe." Margot's best friend Kenzie Foster walked toward her as Harry slithered away to another group. She and Kenzie had been best friends since high school.

"Did you bring the bottle?" Kenzie whispered.

"Yes. I switched it with the identical bottle on the end of the wine tasting table."

"Did anyone see you?"

"Nope. Since the tables are under a tent and no one is supposed to enter yet, I slipped in and out very quickly."

"Is it marked?"

"There's a small black x on the top label. I poured nonorganic red wine into an organic wine bottle. We need to make sure Tessa drinks from that bottle. But just to be certain, we'll do the tasting with her."

"I hope this works."

"It will. After she tastes the marked bottle, I'll distract her while you grab it so no one knows it's not organic red wine."

"I know you want revenge against Tessa, but we need to be careful. I don't want her to *actually* die."

"Don't worry. Tessa will just swell up after drinking it since she has a sulfites allergy. Besides, everything will go as planned."

They made their way to the bar and grabbed a bottled water since they would be tasting wine later.

Tessa, in a flirty, pink designer dress, approached them. Harry by her side. "I see you made it," Tessa said.

"Uh...yeah." Margot glared at Harry.

"I hope you two are ready for a fun evening," Tessa said.

"We're ready," Margot said.

Tessa rubbed Harry's arm. "Harry's not that bad." She purred and sipped her drink with the charm on the glass. She was trying to ruffle Margot's feathers. But Margot wanted no part of it. She had negotiated a generous divorce settlement and used the money to purchase her business. Once she paid Tessa back for her role in the affair, she was free of both of them.

"Great. We'll be starting the tasting soon." Tessa moved away, talking to her guests.

Moments later, Edwin stood near the tent, tapping a fork against a wine glass. "May I have your attention?" He tapped the glass again. "Please gather around."

Guests moved toward Edwin. Tessa stood by his side.

Tessa clapped her hands together. "Welcome to my annual wine tasting. Your mission is to taste each bottle of wine and rate your preference on the card. Then give your card to Edwin so he can tally the results and reveal the most popular wine. Ready. Set. Go!" Tessa headed to the tasting table.

As Margot and Kenzie followed Tessa, Parker Ashby, a realtor and high school friend approached them. "Hey, you two. What cha' up to?"

"Oh...hey Parker," Margot said.

"I'm surprised to see you here after last year's scandal." Parker gripped his glass and sipped his drink.

"That's in the past," Margot said.

"I heard that Harry and Tessa broke up but are back together doing real estate deals."

"Oh really? I'm not privy to what they do," Margot said.

"Good ole' Parker. Always up on the latest gossip." Kenzie smirked and nudged Margot. "We better grab our cards."

"Catch you later?" Margot ducked away from Parker and grabbed Kenzie by the arm. "Uh...sure." Parker turned and followed the crowd to the table.

Margot and Kenzie eased behind Tessa. They sipped and dumped wine in spit buckets, marked preference cards, and chatted with guests while making their way down the line.

"She's approaching the bottle," Margot whispered to Kenzie.

Kenzie stepped closer.

Tessa poured the wine into her glass and tasted it. She leaned against the table. Her face flushed.

"Are you okay?" Margot asked.

"I'm fine. Probably too much wine." Tessa stumbled away. Kenzie grabbed the bottle.

As guests continued to taste the wines and mark their cards, Margot and Kenzie stood by the patio rail by the tent.

"Where's the bottle?" Margot asked.

"I put it in a secure place. We can pick it up later."

Seconds later, a voice called out from the beach. "Help, help!" A woman waved her hands in the air. "Call 9-1-1. Call 9-1-1."

Margot was closest to the dunes and was the first to rush down the stairs and onto the beach. She walked behind the dunes and knelt over Tessa's body. A charm was jabbed into her neck with blood flowing down. The same pink charm from her store. Margot fell backwards, sinking into the sand. "Oh, my God!"

Guests rushed toward the dunes.

Kenzie appeared on the scene. "Tessa!"

*

The medical examiner arrived and transported the body to the morgue. A detective asked guests questions about the turn of events. It didn't help that Margot overheard several of them report her earlier conversation with Tessa. The detective made his way toward Margot who was leaning against the patio rail.

"Margot Berry?"

"Yes."

"I'm detective Tad Hunter. I'd like to ask you a few questions."

Margot nodded.

The detective held a pen and notebook. "I understand you were the first guest to see Mrs. Robinson after the woman walking on the beach found her?"

"Yes."

"According to guests, there was a conversation between you and the deceased?"

Margot frowned. "Tessa was rubbing it in that she and Harry are back together."

"Who's Harry?"

"My ex."

"And why was that?"

"My guess is she thought it would upset me."

"Did it?"

Margot shook her head.

"Did the conversation escalate?"

"No."

"Did you kill Mrs. Robinson?"

Margot's lip quivered. Could he see her tremble? Was he going to arrest her? "No!"

A uniformed officer approached the detective. The men turned from Margot, so she could not hear their conversation. Edwin stood behind them holding a wine bottle.

Detective Hunter faced Margot with the bottle. "What do you know about this?"

Margot shrugged. "It's a wine bottle?"

"Let's refrain from playing games. Edwin informed the officer that you were standing with Tessa at the tasting table. After Tessa walked away, the bottle went missing. What do you know about it?"

Margot hesitated before responding. Had Edwin seen Kenzie hide the bottle? Before she could respond, Kenzie approached them.

"Can I help you?" Detective Hunter asked.

"I was just checking on Margot."

"And you are...?"

"Kenzie Foster."

"Detective Tad Hunter. Nice of you to come...I have some questions for you."

"Me?" Kenzie held her hand against her chest.

"Yes. I was just asking Margot why this bottle was removed from the tasting table."

"I don't know. Why? Is there a problem?"

The detective scratched his head and handed his notebook to Margot. "I need you ladies to write down your names and numbers in case I have further questions."

After the detective walked away, Kenzie turned toward Margot. "Do you think he suspects anything?"

"I hope not."

*

The next morning Margot stumbled out of bed, still shaken over Tessa. Up until now, she'd just wanted to get back at Tessa but had not wanted her killed.

She clicked on the news in her home office and jumped onto the treadmill. The screen flashed, "Local Heiress Murdered." Margot's photo appeared beside it. She grabbed the remote, and turned up the volume. "Margot Berry, owner of The Beach Shop, was questioned by police for the murder of manufacturing heiress Tessa Robinson." The reporter told how Margot was jealous of Tessa and Harry's relationship and how Tessa was found dead behind her estate.

"Omigod!" Margot panicked. Her thoughts raced to Tessa's body in the sand. Why would someone kill her?

*

Three days later, Margot and Kenzie entered the Nags Head Chapel for Tessa's funeral. After signing the guest book, they slipped into a back pew.

"I'm surprised it's an open casket." Kenzie craned her neck for a better view. "Do you want to see Tessa?"

"No," Margot said.

"Well, I do." Kenzie shuffled past Margot and made her way to the front of the chapel.

Margot glanced across the aisle and nodded toward Parker, his eyes red and swollen. She was sure he must be devastated since he and Tessa were good friends and had several real estate deals together. She turned her attention to where Harry sat two rows up.

"I'm surprised to see you here." Edwin stood at the end of the pew.

"My condolences," Margot said.

"I spoke to that detective, and he thinks you had something to do with Tessa's murder. I hope they arrest you soon."

"I didn't murder her!"

Kenzie approached the pew and pushed past Edwin. "The service is starting."

Edwin moved up the aisle and took a seat on the front row.

"Don't let him upset you." Kenzie patted Margot's leg.

*

A few days later, Margot stood behind the counter at her shop retracing the events of the last week. She accessed Tessa's file and viewed the charm receipt. How did the charm end up in Tessa's neck? She glanced at her watch. It was eleven o'clock and she had yet to have one customer. She closed the file and stepped outside onto the wraparound porch. Tourists drove by on Croatan Highway, a main bypass in OBX. The region was a thriving vacation spot with sandy beaches and outdoor activities. Margot wanted to forget about her life and join the fun.

A black jeep pulled into the driveway. Detective Hunter jumped out of it. "I would like to ask you a few questions."

Margot frowned.

He pulled his notebook from his pocket and flipped through the pages. "A receipt was found in Mrs. Robinson's office for cocktail charms. Know anything about that?"

"I sold them to her the day of the event."

"Since this was the murder weapon, you didn't think it was important to mention?"

"I didn't know what to think." Margot steadied herself to keep her legs from shaking.

He fingered another page in the book. "Did you know that Mrs. Robinson only drank organic red wine?"

"Yes. It was due to an allergy."

"But yet there was nonorganic wine found in a bottle according to a lab test."

"Really?" She thought she found just the right tone of surprise.

"Yes, and it has your fingerprints on it and a small x on the label. How do you think that happened?"

"I must have picked it up during the tasting. I'm not familiar with the label. Am I a suspect, detective?" Her heart raced.

"I have to cover all bases and right now you're on first base." He closed the book. "I recommend you hang around OBX. I'll have more questions for you."

*

Since Margot's name had been linked with the murder, business was down at The Beach Shop. With no customers to assist, Margot texted Kenzie about the detective's visit and that she needed to talk to her.

The doorbell jangled. Parker stepped into view. "How's it going?"

"I've been better."

"Yeah. I caught the news. Do the police have any suspects?"

"Other than me?"

"I'm sure they'll come up with something soon." He paused, then added, "I want to talk to you about Harry."

"What about him?"

"Did you know he is one of Tessa's beneficiaries?"

Margot frowned. "What are you talking about?"

"Harry and Tessa were in a deal together to build beach rentals on one of her properties."

"But how would that make him a beneficiary?"

"They had a buy/sell agreement. If something happened to either one of them, the other could buy them out. And they had life insurance on each other to cover the cost."

Margot rubbed her forehead.

"Personally, I think Harry was seeking revenge against her for calling him out about their affair. After all, Harry did pay you a pretty penny during the divorce."

"Are you saying that Harry had something to do with her murder?"

"I don't know." Parker shook his head.

Margot accessed the charm receipt from her computer. "Look at this."

"It's a receipt for three charms. So, what?"

"Tessa was killed with one of the three charms I sold her the morning of the event."

"Really?"

"Yes. Later, at the party, Harry had one charm on his glass, Tessa had one, and the last one ended up in her neck."

"So, you're saying whoever had that last charm is the murderer?"

"Yes. And I intend to find out who that was."

*

The next day, Kenzie stopped by The Beach Shop. "What's up? I got your message."

"The detective stopped by to see me yesterday."

"What did he want?"

"He asked about the charms I sold to Tessa and the bottle of wine that Edwin gave him."

"Do you think he knows we brought the wine?"

"I don't know how since no one saw me switch the bottles. But get this. Parker stopped by and said Harry was in business with Tessa to build beach rentals."

"Really?"

"There's something else. He suspects Harry killed Tessa since they had a buy/sell agreement."

"So, Harry did it?"

"Not sure...but I'm having an after-hours sale and wine tasting at my shop in a few days. I'm inviting some guests from Tessa's party. That way, I can sneak in questions to find out who got the charm. Can you help me?"

"Of course."

*

Three days later, Kenzie helped Margot tag sale items for the after-hours event. They placed wine bottles, beverages, and finger foods on tables throughout the store so that guests could grab items as they browsed the merchandise.

"I hope this works," Kenzie said.

"Me too." Margot hoped the event would bring in the business she had lost due to Tessa's death. The media continued to cover the investigation and Margot disliked the attention and suspicion against her. On a hunch, she hoped to reveal the killer during the party.

"Welcome to The Beach Shop." Margot greeted her customers as they entered the store. She waved her hand toward the sale items and offered food and beverages.

"Hey, there," Parker said.

"Thanks for coming."

"You know me, I'd come to the opening of an envelope." Parker looked around the store. "So, what kind of bargains do you have?"

"All beach items are on sale, home and garden, and wine accessories."

"Speaking of wine, I would love a glass."

As Margot directed Parker to the beverage table, Edwin approached her.

"Look, I'm sorry for being abrupt during the funeral. But when the detective came to see me, I assumed you were guilty since his questions were about you. Plus, I knew you and Tessa didn't have the best friendship."

"What changed your mind?"

"I found out later that Harry had a legal agreement upon her death. And anyone could have brought that bottle of wine. I don't know what to believe so here I am."

Margot realized that Harry might be responsible for Tessa's murder. "I appreciate your honesty, but I have a question."

"What is it?"

"Do you remember a charm with pink beads and metal hooks on Tessa's glass at the party?"

"Yeah, sure. Why?"

"Well...I sold her that charm plus two of the same just before the party. She kept one and gave one to Harry. But do you know who had the third?"

He pressed his finger against his lip. "I do recall seeing one on the bar but don't know who grabbed it. Then of course it ended up in her neck." He lowered his head.

Margot decided not to ask Edwin any more questions. "There's food and beverages throughout the store and the merchandise is displayed."

"Hi," Harry greeted Margot.

"You're always sneaking up behind me."

"It does seem that way. How's it going?"

"I'm trying to get my business back on track and will be glad when they find out who killed Tessa."

"The reading of the will takes place tomorrow."

"Oh really?"

"I'm attending since I'm an investor in a building project with Tessa."

"Tell me. Did you still have a grudge against Tessa? You know, for exposing the affair?"

"No. I just want my money back that I invested. But tonight, I'm here for you." Harry brushed Margot's arm.

Harry wasn't helping the situation since Margot's thoughts ranged from him killing Tessa to her failing business. "There's plenty to eat and drink and merchandise throughout the store."

"Okay. I'll check it out."

Margot headed to the register to ring up merchandise for guests.

"Great turnout," Kenzie said. "Any luck finding out who had the charm?"

"Not yet."

Guests began exiting the store after purchasing items.

Parker approached Margot at the register. "Looks like it's starting to clear out."

"Uh…yeah. Did you find something you like?"

"Do you have any of these charms left?" He held up two starfish charms.

"Of course. I've got some in the back. How many do you need?"

"Two more."

"I need to grab them from the storage room. Be right back."

Margot entered the room and scanned the shelf for the box of charms.

"I thought I would help you." Parker stood behind her, blocking the exit.

Surprised, she turned and faced Parker.

"I knew you were getting close."

"What do you mean?"

"When you showed me the receipt, I knew you would figure it out."

Margot searched his eyes. "You killed Tessa. Why?"

"Because she left me out of real estate deals when she started to do business with Harry. She said I was trying to scam her on the property price. After Harry talked her into using a realtor he knew, I had enough of her using me for free advice and backing out of deals."

"But how did it happen?"

"After I saw Tessa stumble from the table and Kenzie hide the bottle, I knew you were up to something, so I checked on Tessa. She was drunk and lured me down to the beach to chat about Harry. Her face began to swell like she was allergic to something. I've seen it before. We argued, and I stuck her in the neck with the charm from my glass. I panicked but quickly put two and two together that you had poisoned her. That's when I grabbed the bottle of wine and gave it to Edwin."

"You had the third charm?"

"Yes." He stepped closer and wrapped his hands around her neck and squeezed tight. "I killed Tessa, and now I have to kill you."

Margot couldn't breathe. Her eyes bulged from her head. If she didn't do something, she was going to die. She reached into the box and grabbed a charm. She twirled the charm between her fingers and stabbed Parker's arm. He reared back, snarling. Margot ran toward the door.

Parker grabbed her skirt and yanked her to the ground. Margot fell outside the door, landing by the register. Parker jumped on her back and his big hands were around her neck again.

Just as she was blacking out, Parker fell off her back. Margot looked around to see Kenzie whirl an empty wine bottle against Parker's body. Wrenching herself free from the weight of Parker's legs, Margot scrambled to her feet.

Harry and Edwin appeared at the counter, mouths agape as they took in the scene.

Margot raced toward them. "Thank God. Call 9-1-1. Parker just confessed to murder."

*

Two weeks later, Margot stood on a ladder stocking supplies as Kenzie rang items at the register for a customer. With business back on track, she had hired Kenzie due to her attention to detail and ability to think fast on her feet.

The murder of Tessa Robinson had been solved. Detective Hunter had arrested Parker for her murder, but he never solved the wine bottle mystery. Edwin retired after receiving a generous inheritance from Tessa. The rest of the estate went to Tessa's relatives.

The doorbell jangled, and Harry entered the store.

Margot stepped down the ladder. She had one unfinished item of business as she turned off the open sign. "Be right back." She grabbed beverages and glasses in the stockroom.

The three gathered around the counter. Margot mixed the pink cocktail and poured a round. She raised her glass. "For what it's worth…here's to you, Mrs. Robinson."

Harry whispered to Margot. "I don't want you to get away again."

Margot smiled. "Go take that insurance money and build some beach houses."

FROM WHISKEY TO WINE
by Shawn Reilly Simmons

Staci Brew could tell a lot about a person from the poison they picked. Beer drinkers talked louder than necessary, but were generally laid back, and sometimes just plain lazy. Gin devotees thought they were smarter than everyone else, especially the person behind the bar mixing their drink. And anyone who ordered vodka before noon was more than a waving neighbor with the darker side of human nature. The one thing they all had in common was when they had one too many of whatever they chose, they could turn on you faster than a bullet shot from a gun.

And then there were the winos. They were a whole other story all together.

Wine drinkers liked to intellectualize about vintages and harvests, and one up each other on how many different varietals they'd tried. Staci had seen packs of ladies-who-lunch in expensive athleisurewear, polishing it off by the bottle before toddling out the door to pick up their kids from school. Wine was just as potent a drink as any other, it just came in a classier looking bottle.

One thing Staci had learned early, growing up behind the bar at the Cat Scratch Tavern, the establishment her parents had bought the year she was born: No matter what time of day or year it was, the liquor business was a good one. For as long as people have been putting spirits in a bottle, they drink when they're happy, and even more when they're not.

When Alice, the liquor saleswoman that visited the Cat Scratch every week on Wednesdays, up and quit without any notice, Staci applied for her job. Prime Distributors would provide a regular paycheck, something she could show to a mortgage company, cash commission and bonuses, not to mention health insurance, a luxury her parents could only afford on occasion, and something they could really use right now.

Staci took a deep breath and pulled open the door to Jeffrey's, the fanciest bistro on Main Street. The frigid air in the empty dining room chilled the sweat on the back of her neck. She thought about taking off her cropped suit jacket, but instead pulled it tighter over her silky tank top and hitched her sample case further onto her shoulder. The bistro was empty during the lull between lunch and dinner, with only the faint sounds of pans clattering back in the kitchen. A few seconds later Jeffrey, the owner, pushed through the swinging door behind the bar. He stopped short when he saw Staci standing amid the white tablecloths.

"Hi, Jeff."

"You're back," he said. "I wasn't expecting you again so soon."

"I know you said you'd be set for a while, but I've got something special to show you," Staci said, her words tumbling over each other. She fought against the tremor in her hands.

"Really?" Jeff said, wiggling his eyebrows suggestively. "If it's anything like last time..." He chuckled under his breath. "I can't wait to see what else you've got to show me."

Staci cleared her throat. "Something you'll have a hard time forgetting."

His lips stretched into a smile beneath his scratchy mustache. His teeth were tinged yellow from too much wine and coffee. He motioned for her to join him at the bar, then pulled a seat out for her.

"We've just gotten this new wine in," Staci said, perching on the edge of the stool. "And when I tasted it, you're the first person I thought to bring it to." She removed a bottle from her bag and placed it carefully on the bar.

Jeff took his seat and faced her, his legs spread, then reached over and pulled two glasses from behind the bar, and set them in front of her. "What's so special about this wine? I really liked the one we had last week. Is it like that one?"

Staci watched his mustache move up and down as he spoke. She pinched her lips in a smile as she poured him a splash of Burgundy. "You'll see what I mean once you try it. You can tell by the legs that it's got a higher alcohol content. This wine will complement your menu perfectly."

Jeff swirled his glass and observed the purplish bands sliding down the inside of the goblet, then dropped his gaze to Staci's lap. "It does have great legs."

Staci tugged the hem of her skirt a fraction lower and crossed one knee tightly over the other, the toe of her high heel on top of her sample bag. She watched him roll the wine across his tongue. A tangle of veins she hadn't noticed before sprouted on the side of his nose. He glanced at the empty glass on the bar in front of her. "Have some with me."

Staci laughed and shrugged in amused frustration. "This is the only sample bottle I'm allowed. It's a high-end pour, and Ned specifically said the reps should save it for our VIPs. And if he caught us drinking it, we'd get written up."

"Well, we don't want you getting into trouble, do we?" Jeff said. "But I won't tell if you don't."

"What do you think of the wine?" Staci said after an awkward pause.

"I don't know. What else have you got in there?" Jeff glanced down at her bag. "Something you can try with me?"

Staci touched a fingernail to her lip, thinking. Jeff's glance drifted toward the kitchen door and she felt his attention shifting away from her.

"If you don't...I have to get ready for tonight. It's a private event, just one table," he said.

"I think I do have something," Staci said, reaching down and pulling an open bottle of pinot noir from her bag. "This is the one you liked last time."

Jeff settled back onto his stool and nodded at the first bottle. "Tell me more about this high-end pour. It's growing on me."

Staci smiled and poured a more generous amount into his glass. "VIPs always appreciate quality. This soft and subtle light-bodied red comes from the Burgundy region and features gamay grapes. It's got notes of berry followed by a subtle hint of black pepper. This wine is delicious chilled and pairs well with poultry, rabbit, tomato sauces, and most fish."

He admired her for a few seconds before swirling and sipping. No spitting, that wasn't Jeff's style. He said it was a waste of good wine. "How many cases does Ned want you to sell of this?"

"Four," Staci said. "Can I count on you for one or two?"

Jeff closed his eyes and placed his glass on the bar, his mustache twitching. "I might be able to help you out. Except," he paused, and rubbed his chin. "I just brought a bunch of new bottles into the restaurant last month, and got new wine lists printed. I'm not sure we need another Burgundy on the menu, this time of year especially." He glanced out the front window where the late-afternoon sun baked the tops of the cars parked on the street. He pushed his glass a few inches away on the bar.

The door to the kitchen opened a few inches.

Staci poured another finger of wine and pulled the glass back toward him. "I really think this one will work with your gorgeous menu. Give it one last try, now that it's had time to breathe."

"You really need to sell this one, huh?" Jeff said, leaning closer to her. His button-down shirt sagged open at the neck, and she could smell onions on his breath. "I was worried after you left the last time they'd send me a different rep, even though things are going so well. We've built rapport, you and me. Customer service." His words had begun to blur at the edges and his eyelids drooped.

Staci leaned closer to him and smiled, twisting a strand of her long black hair around her finger. "I can really see your place supporting this level of quality wine."

Jeff watched her fingers move through her hair then put his nose in the glass before draining the rest of the wine down his throat. "I'll take all four cases. With the VIP customer service. You have to help me get everything downstairs to the wine cellar." The door to the kitchen closed silently.

Staci's breath caught in her throat and she nodded. "Of course. Anything for a Prime VIP." She pulled a tablet from her sample bag and tapped on the screen. "I'll get these logged in as sales and—"

Jeff grabbed her wrist. "Let's get the wine downstairs now."

Staci pulled against him and laughed playfully. "In a second. I have to get the order in to Ned before cutoff—"

"Jeff." An attractive blond woman in leather pants and stiletto heels stood in the dining room. Jeff let go of Staci's wrist and stood up from the bar, almost knocking the stool over behind him.

"Bev," Jeff said. "Hey, babe. You know...um...the Prime Distributor rep."

"Staci," Staci said as she gathered the wine bottles and her tablet, and zipped up her bag. "Thanks for your order, Jeff. I'll have the guys bring those cases to you with your next delivery." She nodded at Jeff's fuming wife on her way out of the restaurant.

*

Staci sat behind the wheel in her hot car, her heart thumping against her chest. She pulled off her jacket and turned on the car, feeling the whisper of air through the vents blowing against her bare arms. Her phone buzzed on the seat beside her and she looked down and saw her boss's name on the screen. Making no move to answer it, she watched the phone buzz until her eyes blurred.

"Jeff doesn't mean anything by it," Ned had said the morning after in his office. "He's just, you know, overly friendly when he has too much to drink. A little free with his hands."

"Overly friendly?" Staci asked. "He was all over me. He pushed me against the wall in his cellar and...he wasn't taking no for an answer."

Ned's bald head blushed as he laughed nervously. "Jeff told me you came on to him. He actually called to complain about you, said you left before helping him shelve all of the wine he bought in the cellar."

Staci almost leapt from the visitor chair on the other side of Ned's desk. "Yeah, he's right. Because he cornered me, had his hands in my shirt the minute I turned around. Is he crazy? If that chef hadn't come downstairs when he did..."

"Do you want me to take you off the account?" Ned asked, but in a way that made it sound like it was the last thing he wanted to do.

"I don't know."

"The thing is, I gave you a chance here, Staci. Because your parents have been good Prime Distributor customers. You don't have a college degree, and you know with your criminal record it will be hard for you to find something else."

"Criminal record?" Staci asked in disbelief. "I got in the middle of a fight at the Cat Scratch ten years ago. It's been cleared from my record. I was just a kid."

"Still, you took a beer bottle to that guy's head. He had to get stitches," Ned said, running his fat fingers along the edge of his desk.

"Not as many as he'd caused his girlfriend to get over the years," Staci mumbled. "He had his hands around her throat. I was supposed to watch him strangle her?"

"Look, Staci," Ned sighed. "If things are too hard for you here we can—"

"No," Staci said, standing up. "I can handle it."

"Good," Ned said, glancing at her V-neck blouse, which flattered her long neck. "You just have to know how to handle guys like Jeff. Don't lead him on again and hopefully things will be fine. Just don't, you know, put yourself out there so much. It's too tempting for some guys. And I don't want to hear any more complaints about you from Jeff or any other of our customers."

*

The Cat Scratch Tavern's windows vibrated from the live music coming from inside, unable to keep the guitar riffs and drumbeats from escaping into the summer night. Staci yanked the front door open just as a couple came stumbling out, limbs entwined, faces red and shiny.

They made their way to a row of Harleys leaning on their jiffy stands in the dusty parking lot. Staci continued inside, tilting her shoulders to help lug her sample bag through the crowd.

"Where you been?" Staci's mom stood behind the bar, a tie-dyed bandanna covered in skulls wrapped tightly around her head. Her hair was slowly growing back. She only had two more chemo treatments to go before her final round of radiation.

"Long day," Staci shouted over the music. She set her sample case near the cash register and slipped off her jacket. A beer bottle shattered somewhere near the dance floor. "Pop's not back yet?"

"He's on his way. You know how Pop is. He takes his time doing everything."

Staci nodded and kicked off her high heels, slipping on the black Chuck Taylors she kept behind the bar. Even in the flat shoes she still towered over her mom.

"We coulda used you here earlier. We had a big rush, riders coming down the mountain, heading for a rally next town over," her mom said.

"I saw some of them in town," Staci said. She stood for a few seconds with her hands on her hips, looking down at her shoes.

"You okay?" her mom asked, her forehead wrinkling in concern. "You can go home, sweetie. I can handle these lunatics."

"No," Staci said. "I'm here all night."

Her mom shifted in front of the beer faucets to pull a pint for a waiting customer.

Staci grabbed a cocktail shaker and the neck of a vodka bottle from the top shelf, and tilted in a hefty pour over a scoop of ice cubes and a dash of olive brine. Staci shook, then poured the vodka into a chilled martini glass from the refrigerator at her knees. She pierced three olives with a bamboo sword and balanced them on top, then walked it over to the attractive blond woman who'd been staring at her from the end of the bar.

*

Staci sat in one of the booths as her mom counted the cash from the till and her dad swept the floor, clearing away the same debris that was left behind every night. His long gray beard almost touched the floor when he bent over, and his leather vest gathered around his shoulders.

"We sure had a good night," her mom said, tucking the cash into a deposit bag in the back office and locking it in the safe. "I wish they had a bike rally around here every week."

"Mom, come taste this one," Staci said. She eyed the wine glass in front of her and jotted a few notes in her planner. "Tell me what you think it is."

Staci's mom slid into the booth across from her and took a sip. "Sangiovese." The silver rings her mom wore on every finger clinked against the glass.

"Correct again," Staci said with a shake of her head. "It's going to work."

Her mom wiped her brow with the back of her hand. "When you spend your life slinging drinks, you figure out how things taste."

"No, you don't," Staci's dad called from behind the dance floor. "I can't tell a chardonnay from a Coors Light."

Staci's mom waved an annoyed hand in his direction.

"Pop's right," Staci said. "Your palate is perfect."

"That and twenty bucks will get you—"

"Not much at all," Pop called from the other corner of the bar. "Not even a night out at the movies."

Staci rolled her eyes at both of her parents. There was a knock on the front door.

"Closed!" Staci's mom yelled. "Haven't you degenerates had enough to drink already?" Most everyone who frequented the Cat Scratch Tavern was a regular, and a good number of them would self-identify as degenerates. The Cat Scratch didn't get a lot of walk-in business, especially after closing time.

The knock came again, louder this time.

Pop sighed and made his way to the entrance. "Safe's locked?"

"Of course, it is."

Staci's dad puffed out his chest and unlocked the door. "What can I do for you, Sheriff? We're all cleared out. It's just us here."

The sheriff stepped inside the bar and scanned the room, his eyes settling on the wine bottles on the table in front of Staci. "Hi, Pop, Cher. This isn't about serving customers after hours. I'm here to ask Staci a question or two."

Cher put a protective hand on Staci's forearm. "What do you want with our Staci?"

"There's been...well, there's been some trouble in town. And Staci's name came up. It's just routine."

Staci's dad took a step closer to the sheriff, putting his bulky body in between the law man and his family. "What kind of trouble are you talking about?"

The sheriff looked over Pop's shoulder at Staci and her mom. "I hate to tell you this, Pop, but Jeffrey Nickerson is dead. His wife says Staci knows him and was at the bistro earlier."

"Jeff's dead?" Staci asked through numb lips. "How?"

"Drowned," the sheriff said, scraping his boot against the worn wooden floor. "In an ice bucket full of wine."

*

Staci sat in the hallway outside of the sheriff's office wishing she'd had time to change into jeans before coming in for questioning. She was still wearing the short skirt and tank top she'd had on all day. At least she still had on her comfortable shoes.

The door to the office rattled open and Beverly Nickerson strode out, flinging an expensive leather bag over her shoulder. "My husband had a drinking problem," she said to the sheriff who followed her out into the hall.

"My brother does too," the sheriff said. "But he doesn't take naps in ice buckets."

"What might you be implying?" Beverly asked huffily. Despite the late hour, her hair was perfectly styled and her makeup flawless.

The sheriff was at a loss for words.

The two of them stopped in front of Staci.

"Tell him," Beverly said. "Tell him where I was tonight."

Staci crossed her arms tightly. "At the Cat Scratch."

The sheriff chuckled and turned to Beverly. "You a regular at Pop's tavern?"

"Lately, yes," Beverly said. "When you find a bartender who makes a dirty martini exactly right every time, you go back."

"Okay." The sheriff sighed. "And you were definitely there during the time in question, between five and six-thirty p.m.?"

"She was," Staci said. "I served her two martinis."

"And why did you send the chef away from the bistro right before dinner service again?"

"I told you," Beverly said, failing to contain her irritation. We were out of mussels, and Jeff was already...in his cups. I couldn't send him, obviously, and they were on the menu. When Jeff found out I'd sent Chef out instead of him, we had words, and he went to pout in the cellar. He probably decided to drink from the ice bucket instead of coming back up for a glass. That's the one thing about my husband, he never wanted to look bad in front of the staff."

"And no one else was at the restaurant?" the sheriff asked.

"I already told you," Beverly said. "It was a private event. Just Chef and one server and she wasn't due in until right before service at seven. Okay? Can we go now?"

"I'm still trying to figure out how he ended face-down in a bucket full of wine," the sheriff said.

Beverly grimaced. "Obviously, Jeff's drinking finally caught up with him. Alcoholism is a disease, Sheriff. Instead of implying I've done something to my husband, you should be consoling me."

The sheriff contemplated her words silently.

"It's really too much for you to have dragged Staci out at this hour of the night," Beverly continued. "The poor girl is working two jobs. Her mom is fighting cancer. Her parents are long-time business owners in our community. Really, Sheriff, I think there are much better uses of your time and the town's resources."

With a sigh the sheriff nodded. "I think you're probably right. Thank you, ladies, for your assistance this evening. Come on, Staci, I'll drive you home."

"No need," Beverly answered. "I'll give her a lift."

*

Beverly's Lexus purred outside the Cat Scratch Tavern with Staci in the passenger seat. Staci's car was the only one left in the dusty parking lot. The sheriff had driven her into town, even though she told him she'd only sampled the wine from the table.

"How's the rest coming?" Beverly asked. The dash lights glowed, casting them in a deep blue.

"It's ready," Staci said. "The cases will be rotated in and shipped out by the end of the week."

"Perfect," Beverly said. The clock on the dash showed it was just past two in the morning. "Are you going to call in sick tomorrow?"

"Of course not," Staci said. "We've got work to do." She reached for the door handle.

"You know," Beverly said, "I'm really sorry I didn't get to you before…that I didn't warn you about Jeffrey. After what happened to Alice, I should have done something sooner."

Staci gazed at her knees, feelings of anger mixed with confusion, and betrayal a bitter cocktail churning in her stomach. "Why does he do it?"

"He doesn't. Not anymore."

*

Six months later, Staci sat behind her desk at Prime Distributors. The first thing she'd done after Ned's abrupt departure was to have the whole office suite painted pink, reviving the dank yellow walls. She'd read that soft colors were soothing and enhanced productivity.

Prime Distributors, and Ned personally, had avoided any legal trouble stemming from the Jeffrey Nickerson situation, even though

Ned was aware of four Prime employees that had been harassed or worse by his best customer. But he couldn't avoid the scandal that stemmed from Prime knowingly distributing counterfeit wine to their clients. His signature was on all of the purchasing orders, even though he denied knowing anything about the scam.

He never looked at them before signing. The wine tasted just like it was supposed to, even though it was a mixture of lower end table wines, combined to create the illusion of the highest end pours Prime had to offer. Their customers had overpaid by tens of thousands of dollars, and they all sued.

Staci and her mom worked every night after closing on the wines, tasting, and mixing, experimenting with the blends until they were just right. Her dad reinserted the corks and melted the wax. Beverly funded the operation and purchased a good number of the fraudulent cases through her own restaurant, rebranded as Bev's Bistro after Jeffrey's accidental and tragic drowning.

When Ned's options ran out, Beverly's offer to buy Prime was too good for him to pass up. He left quietly, dodging any questions about the harassment or fraud.

Beverly's chef never breathed a word about Pop slipping through the kitchen door as he was on his way out to run Beverly's "errand." He'd picked up some mussels on his way back from sharing a beer with his brother at the corner bar down the street. He enjoyed driving the new Lexus Bev had bought him.

No one had seen Pop in town that day. He'd blended in well with the bikers who had roared through on their way to the rally. The Xanax Staci had slipped in the wine had gone unnoticed. Jeff had accidentally mixed his meds and alcohol on other occasions. Pop found him slumped in a chair, head down on a wooden table. He placed Jeff's face in the ice bucket after filling it with what was left in the open bottles scattered around the cellar.

Bev came into Staci's office, carrying a bottle of Burgundy and two glasses. Staci smiled as the two women toasted their good fortune, and to the future.

THE GOOD CITIZEN
by Mary Dutta

"Again with the raisins." Sylvia tossed the pastry back and rooted through all the others on the platter. "I don't know why they even bother with a suggestion box. I don't think they've read a single suggestion I've put in there."

Ruth moved her plastic tongs away from the pastries and toward a tray of bagels. Sylvia's suggestions, she had noticed, sounded an awful lot like complaints. About everything the senior center offered. Baked goods. Tax assistance. Musical performances. Computer courses. Sylvia groused about them all.

"You're getting glitter in the cream cheese," Sylvia said.

Ruth scraped the gold sparkles out of the tub with a plastic knife and transferred them to her plate.

"I was making posters earlier," she said, gesturing at the community room walls and sending a new shower of gold dust from her clothes onto the tablecloth. Glittery bubbles rose from a drawing of a champagne glass on the nearest poster, which urged the center's patrons to raise a glass to the Good Citizen of the Year at the upcoming award luncheon.

"Let's hope the luncheon champagne is better quality than these baked goods," said Sylvia, as she loaded her plate, bracelets jangling. "You want good champagne you should have been at my daughter's wedding. My first husband was a bum, but he didn't skimp on his little girl's big day. If I told you how much the whole thing cost it would curl your hair."

Ruth was happy with her hair the way it was. And she had been blissfully happy with her late husband, Charlie, who had been the farthest thing from a bum that a person could be. She didn't share either thought with Sylvia, who kept talking as they searched for seats. Ruth waited in vain for someone to wave them over.

"They should give that award to someone who's really contributed to this place," Sylvia said. "You know, my son-in-law installed their new HVAC practically for cost."

Ruth did know. In the time she had spent with Sylvia the past few months, she had heard much about this wondrous son-in-law, and the birthday jewels, cruises, and McMansion he had lavished on Sylvia's daughter. She wondered why his largesse didn't extend to paying someone to do Sylvia's taxes or fix her computer, since she was so dissatisfied with the free services the center provided.

Ruth spied a table. "Are these seats free?" she asked the two women sitting there. Sylvia pulled out a chair without waiting for their response.

The seated women exchanged glances then stood. "We were just leaving," said one, although both of their plates were still half full.

"Please, don't leave," Ruth said, trying to keep the tinge of desperation out of her voice They walked away, leaving her alone with Sylvia.

"Better they shouldn't finish," Sylvia said as she watched them go. "They could both stand to lose a few pounds." Her gaze darted from Ruth's waistline to her plate, and she smiled to herself. Ruth spread her cream cheese with intense concentration.

"May I join you, ladies?" The center director smiled down at them.

"Please," Ruth said, gesturing at the empty chair beside her. "Lovely breakfast, thank you."

"And it's so comfortable in here, isn't it?" said Sylvia, leaning across the table. "I mean, now that the heat is working so well. My son-in-law did such a great job for you. I'm sure the Council on Aging was facing some much higher bids before he stepped in. I hope you all appreciate what we've done for the center."

"If you're talking about numbers," a voice said. "Then I'm guessing you need an accountant."

Ruth made eye contact with the man standing over them, then averted her gaze from his colored contact lenses.

"Don," the director said as the man beamed at them, "you're positively sparkling this morning."

Don gazed down at the glitter on his sleeve. "Poster making," he said. Ruth knew he hadn't been there. He must have dragged his sleeve through the glitter on the food table, probably on purpose. Ruth had met a lot of Dons in her life. The guy who didn't bring notes to the study group but copied everyone else's. The co-worker who signed the group card but didn't chip in for the gift. Last in line to do his part but first in line to claim the credit.

"I'm looking forward to the big announcement," Don said. "Any chance I'm going to be Good Citizen of the Year?"

"You're definitely in the running," the director said. "The Council on Aging really appreciates all our volunteers."

"All of them?" said Sylvia, glaring at Don. "Because let me tell you, one of your volunteers filed my taxes late and cost me a fine." She pointed a lacquered nail at the director. "And whoever is buying all the raisins needs to go."

Ruth put her bagel down. "Sparks always fly when these two get together," she said to the director. "I'm going to head out before things escalate."

In the parking lot, she found Don's car parked next to her own. A roll of toupee tape sat on the passenger seat. Senior center newsletters spilled across the back seat and onto the floor. She leaned against her car and put her head in her hands as a wave of grief washed over her. The newsletters should have been delivered last weekend. She and Charlie had made the rounds every Saturday for years. Unlike Don, her Charlie had been a man of his word. If he said he would do something, he did it. Ruth hadn't recognized just how much he had done until after he died. She had spent many of her newly lonely hours watching YouTube videos learning how to manage home maintenance and handle her finances and look after the car for herself. Charlie had done so much for her, and for the senior center. Don made a sorry substitute.

*

Senior Center Spruce Up Day the next week found Ruth in higher spirits. She looked forward every year to readying the center for the award luncheon. She checked people in on the sign-up sheets she had organized and directed them to the supplies she had arranged. Sylvia had turned up her nose at the notion of work, and Ruth was enjoying her absence. Don hadn't volunteered either, but he was present, chatting with the front desk receptionist and swinging a hammer in one hand. Ruth never saw him actually do anything over the course of the day until the representative from the local Council on Aging arrived, accompanied by a reporter. Don suddenly busied himself rehanging the perfectly level plaque listing past Good Citizen of the Year award winners. Ruth paused on her way to check on a mulch delivery to listen to their exchange. "I've fixed a few loose wires, hammered a few nails," Don was telling the reporter. "There's always work to be done if you know where to look for it."

"Seems like you might be a contender for that award," the reporter said. Don hoisted his hammer and treated her to a view of his bleached teeth as he smiled for her camera. As she set off to interview other volunteers, Don scurried after the Council on Aging representative, who was admiring the range of entertainment options the center provided.

Ruth straightened the plaque Don had left askew. She would need to check on anything else he might have touched in his pretense of helpfulness. She surveyed the names of the previous winners, wishing the award could be bestowed posthumously. Every year, she had waited for Charlie's name to be called. But it never was, and now he was gone. Death was always close at hand in a senior population. Ruth knew well the pain that came with it. It was why she had reached out to Sylvia after the woman's husband died. She had thought that the newly widowed Sylvia was isolated because she, like Ruth, had made her husband her whole world. But in the intervening months, Ruth had come to realize that Sylvia's lack of friends stemmed not from her devotion to her husband but from her painful personality.

Sylvia had seized on Ruth's overtures and insinuated herself into all her activities. She had settled herself behind Ruth's table at the craft fair, offering no crafts of her own and antagonizing all the customers. She attended the book group but never finished the books. She sat next to Ruth at chair yoga and moaned loudly about the discomfort of even the gentlest stretches, and the lack of a hot tub at the center to soothe her aches.

Don showed up for chair yoga, too, always slipping in just after everyone else had finished setting up the chairs. After class, he kept a hand on one chair while he sucked in his stomach and chatted up the limber young yoga teacher, stacking his chair with a flourish after all the others had been put away. Ruth ached for Charlie, who had always been the first to pitch in and the last to leave.

Community theater had never been one of her many interests, but she seized the opportunity to sign up for an outing to a local production when she saw that only one ticket remained. She chatted animatedly with the other seniors as they waited to leave, savoring the respite from Sylvia's company. Her heart sank when Sylvia boarded the shuttle van at the last moment.

"You should have told me you signed up," she said, barreling down the aisle in a cloud of perfume. "I had to promise someone my hairdresser's number to get her to give me her ticket." Ruth slumped in her seat as the two women she had been talking to turned around and started their own conversation.

Sylvia started up again about the need for a hot tub at the senior center. Ruth strained to hear the other women talking about the upcoming Good Citizen of the Year award. They speculated it might go to Don, whose dubious physical charms and ubiquitous presence seemed to have fooled them into believing that he was not only a real catch but a star volunteer.

"He thinks he'll win it," Sylvia interjected, sticking her head between their seats, "but I can tell the Council on Aging some things about your friend Don the so-called accountant that would make their hair stand on end. Besides, they're going to need a new roof soon and they're not going to want to pay full price."

The other women stared at her. Ruth slumped further into her seat.

Sylvia sat back and resumed her monologue. "My daughter has a hot tub at her timeshare. My son-in-law installed it. And I know just the spot for it. That patch of grass behind the flagpole."

Ruth sat up straight. "That's a memorial garden," she said, "a place to remember and reflect. I go there to think about my husband and our life together."

"Eh," said Sylvia, with a dismissive wave, "neither of my husbands was much to write home about."

Ruth turned her head to the window and gazed out at the houses they passed. She and Charlie had planned to spend their lives together in a home like that. But now, Sylvia had somehow strong-armed her way into Charlie's place by her side.

The theater performance was middling, but Ruth didn't expect much better from the talent shows scheduled the next night at the senior center. She dutifully worked behind the scenes to set it up, posting the schedule of acts and laying props out on a table behind a screen.

"Excuse me." Sylvia's raised voice echoed through the community room. She and Don tussled over a karaoke machine. "You broke it," Sylvia said, tapping the dead microphone.

"I fixed it," said Don. "On Spruce Up Day. I reattached the wiring that you pulled loose."

"Fixed it?" Sylvia let out a harsh cackle. "Like you fixed my taxes?"

"I told you to stop complaining to everyone about that," Don glared up at her from where he squatted over the machine.

Ruth paused in her work and watched Sylvia wave the microphone while Don pounded the power button. She edged to the wall and flipped a switch. A sudden flash and a boom erupted from the karaoke machine, and Sylvia and Don both fell to the floor. Don's toupee had been knocked clean off. Ruth watched from behind the screen as people started CPR and called 9-1-1. She turned her back and straightened the props, setting each a precise distance apart.

Given the two deaths, and Sylvia's daughter's lawsuit, the senior center postponed the luncheon and award ceremony. A much quieter affair was held a few months later. Ruth sat with her old friends, the most content she had been since Charlie died. He had never won the Good Citizen of the Year Award that he deserved. But, thanks to all those lonely hours watching YouTube videos on home repair, she had acquired the electrical wiring knowledge to ensure that no one undeserving would win it either.

The center director stepped forward. "Sometimes these awards go to the people who make the most noise, or the biggest demands," he said. "But this year we chose to honor someone for all the unsung, unacknowledged work she does. Please join me and raise a glass to Ruth, our Good Citizen of the Year."

Ruth started as though she'd received an electric shock, then rose to accept the room's applause. She looked at everyone gathered and raised her glass. "To Charlie," she said.

FLY AWAY GOURMET
by Maria Hudgins

"If you have to ask how much it costs, you can't afford it," said no one, ever, on this trip because it truly did not matter to any of them. All were filthy rich except for the pilot, the copilot, the tour director, a magazine editor, and three noted chefs, all of whom had their trip paid for by their employers. The chartered Boeing 757 was fitted with thirty seats that converted into thirty flat beds, luxurious bathrooms, and handwoven carpeting throughout. They were to fly around the world, west to east, stopping over in Paris, Madrid, Athens, and so on, hitting a Five-Star Restaurant in each city. They typically stayed overnight in the city, then proceeded by air to the next city on the following day. This was not a sightseeing jaunt. Hardly anyone was visiting these cities for the first time. This was pure gastronomic indulgence. A wine-lubricated descent into the finest food the world has to offer.

Pilot Gary Nelson, sixty-one but carefully maintaining the body of an athlete, kept his mouth shut, saying nothing that would reveal his opinion of these hedonistic degenerates. He saw them all as a waste of good oxygen. Copilot Mike McDaniel was of a similar opinion, but he wouldn't have been too put off if one of them took a liking to him and offered him a position as their companion.

Tour Director Anna Black, President of Global Adventures, Boston, was by nature a snob of a magnitude that astounded even the oldest families of that Massachusetts city, but she, too, was intimidated by the filthy richness of this group. She found herself cow-towing shamelessly to the guests she was supposed to lead. On this particular leg of their journey—Shanghai to Sydney, Australia— she had set out a fine selection of wines in the galley. A counter arrayed with light hors d'oeuvres was on offer throughout the cocktail hour, which tended to stretch throughout the afternoon or until they landed, whichever came first. Anna actually kept a close eye on wine consumption to avoid delivering guests to their dinner already three sheets to the wind.

Seats were widely spaced with room to get up and walk around. Anna saw that most travelers were seated and looked as if they were ready for the wine of the day. Today's wine—a special treat— was a 1995 Screaming Eagle Cabernet Sauvignon. Not for sale anywhere because the entire vintage had sold out years ago, but a case or two still sat, undisturbed, in the cellars of Ocaso, the San Francisco restaurant of Chef Nate Martinez. Nate had relieved the restaurant of six bottles of Screaming Eagle and was now pouring small glasses to serve to the airborne group. No one aboard was so crass as to mention that this stuff had sold for three thousand dollars a bottle when it could be sold at all. Now it was priceless.

Three women from Miami, all wives of men connected somehow with jai alai and gambling, sat expectantly in their butter-soft leather seats around a low table, as they had heard about this legendary wine they were about to be served.

Mike McDaniel stood in the doorway to the cockpit, perhaps longing to sample the wine himself, but strictly forbidden by company rules to take even a sip.

Olivia Bissette, feature editor of *Cuisine* magazine, sat on the starboard side of the cabin taking notes on an iPad. She wore a navy pencil skirt, white blouse, and red Jimmy Choo shoes. She looked up briefly when Nate approached with a tray of small tulip glasses. She lifted one off the tray without looking at Nate or even pausing in her note-taking. But she drew back suddenly when Nate dropped his tray. It clattered against the edge of Olivia's chair, as he clapped his hands in the air above his head.

"Mosquito!" he muttered and hastened to apologize to Olivia, whose navy skirt, fortunately, barely showed the wine at all. Several passengers groaned at the loss of three lovely glasses of 1995 Screaming Eagle Cabernet Sauvignon. As each one sipped, they held their small glass up to the light and whispered their first impression. "Plum. Smoke. Blackberry. Cloves."

Someone asked, "How did a mosquito get in here?"

Someone else said, "It would have to be a 'shanghaied' mosquito, wouldn't it?"

A serious discussion about Japanese seafood between Victoria Crawley and Barry Epstein, paused at the disturbance, but only briefly. Both were renowned chefs—Victoria from London, Barry from New York. They were recalling their group's evening at the restaurant in Tokyo when both of them had thrown caution to the wind and ordered the fugu fish. Victoria was a bit tipsy already. She admitted that the best thing about fugu was the suspense, waiting for that tingling on the tongue that could mean the chef hadn't properly cleaned out the liver and you might be about to die. Barry suggested the occasional report of a customer dying after eating fugu was more for publicity than anything else. People do love to feel as if they are taking a risk.

Their first stop on the flight around the world had been Paris, where they had been guests of the owner of a quaint little restaurant on the Left Bank. They had chosen their entrées ahead of time to avoid stressing the kitchen beyond its capacity. Next came moussaka in Athens, then seafood in Tokyo, and crab dumplings in Shanghai. This evening it would be lamb shanks in Sydney.

Nate cleaned up the wine spill himself, using a spray bottle of cleaner Anna found in the galley. As he knelt on the carpet, two members of the group stood over him sighing sadly at the loss of the irreplaceable vintage. Anna decided they had started happy hour too early since they wouldn't land in Sydney for another hour and a half. Meanwhile, she straightened up the galley while most of the group reclined their seats and took a nap. She started to throw away the empty bottles. Nate had opened and used two bottles of Screaming Eagle. Both now sat, empty, on the counter. She wondered if she might save one as a keepsake, then remembered they were less than halfway through their three-week jaunt. She didn't care to keep track of an empty bottle for that long.

Five o'clock and time to wake them all up: Anna stepped up to the sound system near the galley and selected an album of Australian music. "Waltzing Matilda" started out softly, then grew slowly louder as Anna twisted the volume knob. The sleepers began to stir and the readers checked their watches. "Welcome to the Land

Down Under," she purred into the mike. "Don't worry. We have plenty of time before we land. If you want to freshen up or change for dinner, you can do so." She wandered back through the cabin, checking to make sure everyone was awake.

And everyone was, except Olivia Bissette. Anna called her name softly, then touched her shoulder. Olivia slumped sideways in her chair, then fell to the floor. Her iPad hit the floor near her right arm. Everyone snapped to attention at the swoosh Olivia's body made as it slid to the carpet. Anna knelt beside the editor's inert form, mumbling, "Oh, no, omigod, oh please no!" She started to slap Olivia's face, and then thought better of it. Wouldn't look right. Call a doctor? Check her pulse. Anna grabbed the inert woman's left wrist hoping for a pulse, but felt nothing.

She lowered her head to Olivia's face. No sign of breath. Now what? Anna felt her body being shifted to one side.

"Step back, everybody." Captain Gary Nelson walked in and knelt beside Olivia. He rolled her body onto her back and motioned for others to move books and purses that were in his way. For the next few minutes, he administered CPR while his passengers looked on. At length, he stopped. "She's gone," he said.

Copilot Mike dragged a wheeled stretcher from a storage space and helped Captain Gary lift the body onto it. They reclined the hindmost seat in the cabin and moved Olivia on it. Fortunately, the plane was stocked with a number of movable curtains for passengers who preferred privacy, so the two pilots pulled one around the bed and left her to rest in peace.

Next, Anna needed attention. She had passed out cold. One of the passengers, a former nurse and now the wife of a social media magnate, took charge and brought her around with a bottle of something she found in the cabin's first aid kit.

The group members found their voices and began debating. "Did she have any conditions?" one asked.

"Who talked to her this morning?"

"Was she feeling bad?"

Anna motioned for someone to bring her briefcase. In it, she found a folder with everyone's emergency information. She retrieved her glasses from under a table and read the sheet Olivia, like everyone else, had submitted before the trip. "Nothing," she said. "No problems."

"What about that wine?" someone said.

"The Screaming Eagle?" someone else said.

Nate Martinez stiffened. It had been his wine. "I assure you, there was nothing wrong with the wine."

"How do you know?"

"I had a taste of it myself before I served it. Truth be told, I had two of those little glasses before I...well, I figured I deserved it. My restaurant is paying for it." He looked around at the assembly of intent faces. "Okay. Sorry. That sounded rude. I'm just so...I can't believe what just happened."

"Did you sample both of the bottles you served or just one?" Chef Barry Epstein said. "It doesn't matter because here's the thing. It wasn't the Screaming Eagle or we'd all be sick...or maybe just half of us, if there was something wrong with one bottle but not the other."

"What was Olivia drinking before you came around with the Screaming Eagle?"

"Same thing I was drinking," said Victoria, now apparently stone sober. "I opened the bottle of Pinot Gris myself. Nothing wrong with it."

Someone near the bulkhead muttered, "And if there had been something wrong with it, you'd already downed enough to kill you."

Others shifted uncomfortably. This was no time for snide remarks.

Victoria ignored the comment and said, "We need to get all the bottles tested. All of them. They're all in the trash bin and they'll have a bit left in them. Let's pull them all out and cork them until we can figure out what to do next."

"There will be labs in Sydney," someone said. "Forensic labs."

"Wait a minute," Barry said. The New York chef's voice sounded firm and sensible. "It can't be the wine unless there's a bottle in the galley that only she drank from. If any of us had drunk from the same bottle, we might not be dead, but we'd at least be sick. Olivia did not drink a whole bottle herself, so unless there's a half-full bottle in the galley—"

"Were there any bottles already open when we started our cocktail hour?"

At last, Anna found her voice. "No. I opened them all myself, except for the one Victoria opened. There were none already open."

"It's hard to see how anyone could have tampered with the wine."

"Hard? No. Impossible," Anna said.

"If not the wine, then what?" one of the jai alai wives said.

"I'm thinking fugu." Victoria stopped everyone cold with this comment.

"From Tokyo?" The former nurse who was still sitting with Anna said, "That was three days ago. Fugu poisoning doesn't hang around for three days before making you sick. If it's going to kill you, it kills you—" She snapped her fingers.

"How about the dinner in Shanghai?" a former U.S. Senator asked.

"Again. Most of us had the dumplings and we're not sick," the woman next to him said.

"Back to fugu," Victoria said. "Simple food poisoning doesn't kill you, and it doesn't wait a whole day to start. Unless we find out this was a heart attack or something, it must have been a powerful, deadly, poison!" She shivered as she said it.

Several in the group reached for their iPads and laptops. The plane's WiFi was state-of-the-art. They were all Googling "fugu." Now and again a finger would go up when someone thought they had something important.

Copilot Mike slipped out of the cockpit and found Anna. He whispered, "The captain has radioed ahead for an ambulance. They want us to stay aboard until they can—remove—that is—you know—the body."

"Okay. Can you tell him to also radio the Moonstone restaurant in Sydney and tell them we're going to be late?" Anna said.

Mike hesitated, thinking it seemed callous to go to a great restaurant so soon after this tragedy, realized a dinner of airport food would serve no purpose, then promised to make the call.

*

Victoria made her way to the curtained-off area in the back of the plane where Olivia's body lay. She'd had no special liking for Olivia since, like most well-known chefs, she had been stung by the editor's published reviews. But still, she felt she should make sure Olivia's last public appearance (from the plane to the waiting ambulance) would not be marred by an embarrassing blouse unbuttoned or legs spread akimbo. The first thing she noticed inside the curtain was Olivia's red Jimmy Choo shoes on the floor. Stiletto heels. How could she wear those all day? Long years on hard kitchen floors had rendered Victoria's feet incapable of tolerating anything but orthopedic slip-ons. She picked up the shoes and clacked them together, absently. Something was gnawing at her. Shoes. Something about shoes. Recently. A few minutes ago.

It wouldn't come to her.

Victoria shifted Olivia's body slightly and straightened the legs. A tiny drop of blood, now dried, clung to the side of Olivia's left leg, just above the ankle. Did that mosquito Nate swatted do this? Mosquito bites don't normally bleed, but they do redden the skin around the area. She looked closer and spotted an almost invisible puncture. She wondered if it would be possible to find that mosquito. It might still be lying on the carpet near Olivia's seat. Could it have been carrying something deadly?

Satisfied that Olivia looked presentable, Victoria stepped through the curtain and down the aisle between the leather seats.

Nate Martinez's feet were up, his footrest extended. Nate had changed his shoes. Victoria distinctly remembered he had been wearing leather topsiders earlier, but now he wore canvas sneakers. If he had changed for dinner, why had he gone from deck shoes to the more casual sneakers?

She reversed her path and returned to the rear of the plane where several group members had stowed their day packs against the bulkhead. Nate's topsiders lay side by side beneath his dark green backpack. She pulled them out and noticed that the right shoe had been altered. The stitches between the leather upper and the rubber sole was missing for about a half inch at the toe, leaving a small gap that opened a bit when she squeezed the leather. It was the sort of flaw that might develop in older shoes whose stitching had worn through, but these shoes were practically new.

Victoria slipped quietly back to her seat next to Barry Epstein, who was still surfing the web on his laptop. "Let's talk."

By this time, Barry knew enough that he could say for certain the fugu Olivia may or may not have eaten three nights ago could not be the reason she died. The timing was all wrong.

Victoria told him about the shoes and the tiny drop of blood on Olivia's leg.

Barry's face screwed up as if in horror. "Okay. What if it wasn't a mosquito at all? I'm thinking poison dart...oh, I don't know...I read a story once...too weird!" Barry slapped his own face. He glanced around. Nate Martinez was watching him. "Let's go to the bathroom. Together."

Victoria was old enough to realize this wasn't a come-on from the young Barry Epstein. She followed him at a discreet distance to the bathroom near the cockpit, but left an interval of a minute or so to make it less likely anyone would realize the room was already occupied. In those cramped quarters, the two chefs from opposite sides of the Atlantic worked it out and decided there was a needle somewhere on that plane. A needle covered in the potent poison of the fugu fish.

Stepping out again, Victoria saw that Nate had left his seat. Behind her, Barry was leaning against the tiny bathroom sink, his face nearly bloodless. "Uh oh." She hoped he wasn't about to pass out like Anna.

She marched to the back of the plane where she found Nate pushing frantically on an emergency exit. "I wouldn't do that, Nate. You don't have a parachute." Silly as this sounded, it was all she could think of. But Nate, in a blind panic, was helpless to read or follow the instructions on how to open the door.

Instead, he let out a sort of howl and crumbled into a heap beside a pile of backpacks and purses.

*

They found the needle wrapped in toilet paper in the aft bathroom. Pulling out the whole plastic bin liner, a cleaner at the airport made them all stand back until a man from airport security, following a safety protocol he had just made up, extracted the needle, paper and all, and transferred it to an evidence bag.

Nate was detained at airport security, pending the arrival of Sydney Police and Australia Federal Police. The rest of the group hopped into waiting limousines.

The group had lost its appetite, but they went on to the Moonstone to avoid letting the restaurant down. Barry Epstein filled in the missing information they all wanted—the motive. Why had Nate done it?

"Nate was more than just the chef at his restaurant," he told them. "He was also the owner. Sole owner, in fact, since his partner died. Business has been horrible since Olivia Bissette's review came out. She had trashed the place. She insinuated the Ocaso served food that wasn't just bad—it was unsafe. She suggested—without any proof—that Nate was picking up discarded seafood at the waterfront. FDA investigators have found no evidence of this but what's done is done. Olivia's magazine has ordered her to print a retraction but hey, y'know?"

Murmurs drifted around the table. Victoria glanced at Barry, then turned to the waiter. "I'll have the Lamb Shanks."

Almost everyone ordered the Lamb.

Nobody ordered fish.

ACKNOWLEDGMENTS

The authors would like to thank Teresa Inge and Heather Weidner for their time and talent in coordinating the book. We appreciate all their work on this project. We would also like to thank Untreed Reads for publishing *Murder by the Glass*.

AUTHOR BIOS

BETSY ASHTON, born in Washington, DC, was raised in Southern California where she ran wild with coyotes in the hills above Malibu. She is the author of the Mad Max Mystery series, *Unintended Consequences, Uncharted Territory*, and *Unsafe Haven*. She published her stand-alone serial killer psychological suspense novel, *Eyes Without a Face*, in 2017, and her literary effort, *Out of the Desert*, came out in August 2019. Her short stories and poetry have appeared in several anthologies including *50 Shades of Cabernet, Candles of Hope*, and *Reflections on Smith Mountain Lake*. She is the past president of the state-wide Virginia Writers Club.

Social media links:
http://www.facebook.com/betsy.ashton
http://www.twitter.com/betsyashton
http://www.instagram.com/betsy_ashton2005

FRANCES AYLOR (www.francesaylor.com) won the IngramSpark Rising Star Award for her first novel, *Money Grab*. A Chartered Financial Analyst, she is a past president of CFA Society of Virginia and gives presentations on money management. A member of International Thriller Writers and president of Sisters in Crime–Central Virginia, she is an avid traveler who has paraglided in Switzerland, gone white-water rafting in Costa Rica, and fished for piranha in the Amazon. Her short stories appear in *Deadly Southern Charm* and several other anthologies.

Contact her at:
fjaylor@hastingsbaycapital.com
Facebook: https://www.facebook.com/FrancesAylorAuthor/
Amazon: https://www.amazon.com/Frances-Aylor/e/B071CX9HQ8

MARY DUTTA traded New England and a career as an English professor for a job in college admissions in the South. She is the winner of the New England Crime Bake Al Blanchard Award for her short story "The Wonderworker," which appears in *Masthead: Best New England Crime Stories*. Her work can also be found in the anthologies *The Fish That Got Away* and *The Best Laid Plans: 21 Stories* of *Mystery & Suspense*. She is a member of Sisters in Crime and the Short Mystery Fiction Society.

Follow her on Twitter: @Mary_Dutta

DIANE FANNING is the Edgar-nominated author of 15 true crime books and 11 mysteries. She has served as a consultant to *48 Hours*, as a regular presence on 13 seasons of *Deadly Women*, and appeared on the *Today Show*, *20/20*, *Forensic Files*, *Snapped*, the Biography Channel, *Investigation Discovery*, E! and the BBC, as well as numerous cable network news shows and radio stations across the States and Canada. Raised in Baltimore, she moved to Virginia, then south Texas, and she now lives in the shadow of the Blue Ridge Mountains in Bedford, Virginia. http://dianefanning.com

Judge DEBRA H. GOLDSTEIN writes Kensington's Sarah Blair mystery series (*Four Cuts Too Many*, *Three Treats Too Many*, *Two Bites Too Many*, *One Taste Too Many*). She also wrote *Should Have Played Poker* and IPPY Award–winning *Maze in Blue*. Her short stories have been named Agatha, Anthony, Derringer finalists. Debra's short story "Thanksgiving in Moderation," was featured in Untreed Reads' anthology *The Killer Wore Cranberry: A Fourth Meal of Mayhem*. She serves on the national boards of Mystery Writers of America and is president of SEMWA. She previously was on Sisters in Crime's national board and president of SinC's Guppy Chapter.

Find out more about Debra and sign up for her newsletter at:
https://www.DebraHGoldstein.com
Follow her on Twitter: (@DebraHGoldstein)
BookBub: https://www.bookbub.com/profile/debra-h-goldstein
Facebook: https://www.facebook.com/DebraHGoldsteinAuthor/

LIBBY HALL is a Communications Analyst for a Richmond, Virginia, consulting firm, which pays for her horse, bourbon, and book habits. But her real jobs are wife, mother, and fiction/blog writer. You can find her real thoughts about life on her Subourbonmom.blog. Her short story "Stewing" can be found in the *Deadly Southern Charm* mystery anthology.

MARIA HUDGINS is the author of four Dotsy Lamb Travel Mysteries, *Death of an Obnoxious Tourist*, *Death of a Lovable Geek*, *Death on the Aegean Queen*, and *Death of a Second Wife*. These stories are set in Italy, Scotland, the Greek Islands, and Switzerland, respectively.

Before using a place as a setting, Hudgins visits and takes copious notes. Two mysteries in her new Lacy Glass Series are now available on Kindle and Kindle Prime. *Scorpion House* centers around an expedition house in Luxor, Egypt. *The Man on the Istanbul Train* follows the young botanist from Istanbul to an archaeological dig in central Turkey. She lives in Hampton, Virginia.

TERESA INGE grew up reading Nancy Drew mysteries. Combining her love of reading mysteries and writing professional articles led to writing short fiction and novellas.

Today, she doesn't carry a rod like her idol but she hot rods. She juggles assisting two busy executives at a financial firm and is president of the Sisters in Crime, Mystery by the Sea chapter. Teresa is the author of the *Virginia is for Mysteries Series*, *50 Shades of Cabernet*, *Mutt Mysteries Series*, and *Coastal Crime Mysteries by the Sea*.

She resides in Southeastern Virginia with her husband and two dogs. **She can be reached on all social media or by posting a comment on her website:** www.teresainge.com.

ELEANOR CAWOOD JONES read *Ellery Queen Mystery Magazine* at a young age. She began writing in elementary school, using #2 pencils to craft crime stories starring her stuffed animals.

Her stories include "Keep Calm and Love Moai" (Malice Domestic 13: *Mystery Most Geographical*), "All Accounted for at the Hooray for Hollywood Motel" (Bouchercon's *Florida Happens*), and Derringer Award–winning "The Great Bedbug Incident and the Invitation of Doom" (*Chesapeake Crimes: Invitation to Murder*).

A former newspaper reporter and reformed marketing director, Eleanor is a Tennessee native who lives in Virginia and travels often. You'll find her rearranging furniture or lurking at airports.

MAGGIE KING is the author of the Hazel Rose Book Group mysteries, including *Murder at the Book Group* and *Murder at the Moonshine Inn*. Her short stories appear in *Virginia is for Mysteries, 50 Shades of Cabernet*, and *Deadly Southern Charm*.

Maggie is a founding member of Sisters in Crime Central Virginia, where she manages the chapter's Instagram account. Maggie graduated from Rochester Institute of Technology with a degree in Business Administration and has worked as a software developer and a retail sales manager. She lives in Richmond, Virginia, with her husband, Glen, and two mischievous cats. http://www.maggieking.com

KRISTIN KISSKA used to be a finance geek, complete with MBA and Wall Street pedigree, but now she is a self-proclaimed *fictionista*. Kristin contributed short stories of mystery and suspense to nine anthologies, including *Deadly Southern Charm* (2019). She is a member of International Thriller Writers, James River Writers, and is the Vice President of the Central Virginia chapter of Sisters in Crime. Kristin lives in Virginia with her husband and three children.

When not writing, she can be found on:
Her website: *KristinKisska.com*
Facebook: *KristinKisskaAuthor*
Tweeting: *@KKMHOO*
Instagram: *@kristinkisskaauthor*

ALLIE MARIE is the author of the award-winning historical mystery books in the "True Colors Series," as well as a standalone sequel *Return to Afton Square*. She has tried her hand at various genres with several short stories, including a very "outside her comfort zone" fantasy adventure, Amazon bestseller *Tournament of Reckoning*.

Retired from law enforcement, she is currently working on her first crime thriller novel, as well as the "True Spirits Trilogy," a spin-off of her first series. When not writing, she enjoys traveling and camping with her husband. **Allie can be found on FB at** https://www.facebook.com/Author-Allie-Marie-846744515375049

K.L. MURPHY is a freelance writer and editor and the author of the Detective Cancini Mystery Series: *A Guilty Mind, Stay of Execution* and *The Last Sin*. Her short story, "Burn," is featured in the anthology *Deadly Southern Charm*. She is a member of International Thriller Writers, Sisters in Crime, James River Writers, and Historical Writers of America. She lives in Richmond, Virginia, with her husband, children, and two amazing dogs. **She can be found at** www.kellielarsenmurphy.com.

ALAN ORLOFF is a two-time winner of the ITW Thriller Award. He's also won a Derringer Award, been a finalist for both the Shamus and Agatha Awards, and had a story selected for *The Best American Mystery Stories* anthology. His story "Sex Kills," appears in the Anthony Award–nominated anthology *The Beat of Black Wings*, published by Untreed Reads. His latest novel, *I Play One On TV*, a YA thriller, came out recently from Down & Out Books. www.alanorloff.com

JOSH PACHTER was the 2020 recipient of the Short Mystery Fiction Society's Golden Derringer Award for Lifetime Achievement. His crime stories have been appearing in *Ellery Queen's Mystery Magazine, Alfred Hitchcock's Mystery Magazine,* and many other periodicals and anthologies since the 1960s. He also edits anthologies—recent titles include *The Beat of Black Wings: Crime Fiction Inspired by the Songs of Joni Mitchell* (Untreed Reads, 2020), *The Misadventures of Nero Wolfe* (Mysterious Press, 2020), and *The Great Filling Station Holdup: Crime Fiction Inspired by the Songs of Jimmy Buffett* (Down and Out Books, 2021)—and translates fiction and nonfiction from Dutch (and other languages) to English. He lives outside Richmond with his wife Laurie.

SHAWN REILLY SIMMONS is the author of *The Red Carpet Catering Mysteries* and of over a dozen short stories appearing in various anthologies.

Shawn's story "The Last Word" won the Agatha in 2019, and she was nominated for an Anthony Award as co-editor of the anthology in which it appeared, *Malice Domestic 14: Mystery Most*

Edible. Shawn serves on the Board of Malice Domestic, is an editor at Level Best Books, and is a member of Sisters in Crime, Mystery Writers of America, the International Thriller Writers, and the Crime Writers' Association. She lives in historic Frederick, Maryland.

Socials:
Facebook: @ShawnReillySimmons
Twitter: @ShawnRSimmons
Pinterest: @ShawnSimmons
Instagram: @ShawnRSimmons

HEATHER WEIDNER writes the Delanie Fitzgerald mysteries. Her short stories/novellas appear in *Virginia is for Mysteries, 50 Shades of Cabernet, Deadly Southern Charm,* and The Mutt Mysteries. Her new cozy series, the Jules Keene Glamping Mysteries, launches October 2021. She is a member of Sisters in Crime (Central Virginia, Chessie, Guppies), ITW, and James River Writers.

Heather, a Virginia Beach native, has been a mystery fan since Scooby-Doo and Nancy Drew. She lives in Midlothian with her husband and a pair of Jack Russell terriers. Through the years, she has been a cop's kid, technical writer, college professor, software tester, and IT manager.

Contact Information:
Website and blog: http://www.heatherweidner.com
Twitter: https://twitter.com/HeatherWeidner1
Facebook: https://www.facebook.com/HeatherWeidnerAuthor
Instagram: https://www.instagram.com/heather_mystery_writer/